# Just a Bit Heartless

Straight Guys Book 13

Alessandra Hazard

# Table of Contents

# Chapter 1

"The boss is expecting you. Good luck."

Jordan Gates gave the secretary a faint smile before opening the door and going inside.

There were very few things Jordan disliked as much as being called to his boss's office. As a department head, he saw him more often than the average employee, but being unexpectedly summoned to Raffaele Ferrara's office was never a good sign. Thankfully, it hadn't happened all that often in the years that he'd worked for the company.

Jordan came to a halt, his face carefully schooled into a mask of polite attention as Ferrara looked at him from across the desk.

"Sit," Ferrara said tersely.

Jordan didn't take the tone personally. Ferrara's abrupt, harsh manner was rather legendary. The vice president of the Caldwell Group wasn't one for small talk.

Jordan sat down in one of the chairs. "You wanted to see me, sir?" Ferrara was just a year older than he was, thirty-three, but his very presence seemed to demand respect, so it wasn't all that off-putting to have to address his peer as sir. Ferrara had men twice his age addressing him that way.

His boss regarded him for a moment, his black eyes rather unnerving—if Jordan were prone to feeling unnerved.

"I need your help."

Jordan blinked. Until now, he had been sure those words weren't in his boss's vocabulary. "Of course. How can I help?"

Ferrara folded his hands on the desk, his expression sharp and assessing.

Meeting his gaze calmly, Jordan kept himself still as the silence stretched. He refused to let Ferrara intimidate him.

"You might have heard of the incident that happened to me three days ago," Ferrara said at last.

Jordan raised his eyebrows. Incident? That was what Ferrara was calling an attempted murder? The entire company had been buzzing with speculation since someone had shot Ferrara. The bullet had just grazed his head, but there was still a lot of blood, and yet Ferrara was back at work the next day as if nothing had happened. The man truly was a workaholic.

"I've heard," Jordan said dryly. He didn't think there was anyone in Boston who hadn't heard of it. Ferrara was one of the most successful businessmen in the city. It didn't help that he was heavily rumored to have family links to the Italian mafia—the rumor that had been around for years and was a hot topic again.

"What you don't know is that it was the third attempt on my life this month," Ferrara said, his tone mild, as if he were talking about the weather.

Third?

Ferrara pinched the bridge of his nose and leaned back in his chair. "There's more," he said with obvious reluctance. "There has been a kidnapping attempt on Nate."

Jordan frowned. It was widely known in the company that Nate Parrish was Ferrara's lover.

It had been a subject of much gossip last year. Although fraternization in the company was frowned upon, it wasn't forbidden as long as it wasn't within the same department. People still gossiped, of course. A lot of people disapproved, considering that Nate had been Ferrara's PA before he was transferred to Jordan's department to work as a level designer. Personally, Jordan didn't give a shit. Nate was a good dev and he got the job done. Jordan didn't care if Nate was also sucking their boss's cock.

But apparently some people did care—cared enough to attempt to kidnap him.

"Because of your relationship?" Jordan said in a neutral voice.

Ferrara grimaced before giving a clipped nod. "We presume it's related to the assassination attempts on me. Nate doesn't have enemies. I do."

"You don't mean business enemies, do you?" Jordan said quietly.

Ferrara shrugged, his expression hard and grim. "I don't know for sure. But I presume it has something to do with my family. With my father. He died two months ago. Shot in the head."

Huh.

Jordan didn't bother offering condolences. Ferrara didn't want empty condolences. He wanted something else. The question was, what.

Leaning back in his chair, Jordan pondered it. Maybe the rumors were true and Ferrara's father had been some big shot in the mafia. But as far as Jordan knew, Ferrara was estranged from his family in Italy, had been for years. Why was this happening now? What did they want with Nate?

More importantly, what did Ferrara want with *him*? Why was he telling him all of this? Raffaele Ferrara was a very private man. Jordan could count on his fingers the number of times his boss had spoken of something remotely personal over the years, much less about something as deeply personal as the death of his father.

"May I speak freely?" Jordan said.

Ferrara gave a clipped nod.

"What sort of help do you need from me?" he said. "It's obviously not financial. Nor is it likely that you want my advice. We're hardly close friends." He tapped his chin with his knuckles, thinking. "It has something to do with Nate, doesn't it?"

"Yes," Ferrara said. "I was invited to the wedding of my cousin in Italy—or rather, me and Nate. I could decline the invitation, of course, but I don't think that would be smart. The assassination attempts won't stop if the issue isn't resolved. So I accepted the invitation. That's where you come in."

Jordan stared at him as the realization sank in. "You want me to pretend to be Nate," he said incredulously.

"You look similar enough," Ferrara said.

Jordan frowned.

He supposed that was true enough. Although Nate was younger by quite a bit, they had a similar build and facial features, as well as blond hair and blue eyes. Jordan's hair was a few shades darker, but that was nothing some hair dye couldn't fix. At a passing glance, they could probably be mistaken for one another—if one didn't know them personally and if Jordan didn't wear his hair styled and slicked back.

"The resemblance wouldn't fool airport authorities," he stated.

"It doesn't need to fool them," Ferrara said, unfazed. "Nate will accompany me to Italy. You will arrive on a different plane and switch places with him after he gets through customs."

Jordan couldn't help it: he chuckled. "I feel like I woke up in a Bond movie."

Ferrara didn't even crack a smile, his gaze serious. Grim.

The smile died on Jordan's lips.

"I will not lie to you," Ferrara said, his voice quiet. "It will be dangerous. You will be walking into a situation that I can't entirely predict or control. We will stay at my family's estate for a week. There will be other guests there. Dangerous guests."

Jordan's mouth was dry. "Dangerous—as in they play dangerous mind games, or dangerous as in they might shoot me between my eyes?"

"Both," Ferrara said.

Right.

That was…

"Right," Jordan said, clearing his throat. "So you want to take me with you because you aren't willing to risk Nate's safety." *And you are totally fine risking mine.*

"Yes," Ferrara confirmed. "But not only. Nate is—too nice and kind. Some people in my extended family would eat him alive, even if there weren't the danger of someone literally killing us. You're not too kind or nice. You're also very observant and composed. I will need your help in order to find out who wants me dead and why. And if things go south, it also helps that you box and you know how to handle a gun. I trust that you can take care of yourself."

Jordan quashed down the urge to feel flattered.

It was far more likely that Ferrara wouldn't worry about him because he didn't care for him. Nate and concern for his safety would be a distraction for Ferrara; he simply didn't give a damn about Jordan. Ferrara was a cold bastard who was probably just manipulating him into accepting. Jordan also was a little creeped out that his boss was aware of his hobbies: it wasn't common knowledge that he boxed and was good with a gun.

"Why don't you just go alone if you don't want to risk Nate's safety?" Jordan said.

Ferrara leaned back in his chair, loosening his tie a little. "You have to understand how unusual it is that Nate was also invited. I haven't spoken to most of my family in over a decade. I certainly didn't tell any of them about Nate. Which means someone from my extended family is keeping tabs on me. That someone is very likely to be the same person trying to kill me. Even if someone recognizes that you aren't Nate, that would be useful too: it would give us a clue as to who has been keeping tabs on me. Besides, leaving Nate behind would make him an easier target and I'm not comfortable with the thought of being an ocean away if something happens to him."

Jordan couldn't argue with that logic.

"You don't have to agree," Ferrara said. "I wouldn't hold that against you, because you would be putting your life at risk. But if you help me, you will be rewarded for your trouble, of course. You'll be paid your annual salary for this."

Jordan struggled not to show his surprise. As head of a small department, he did pretty well for himself. He couldn't deny that it was incredibly tempting to earn his yearly salary in a week. But for Ferrara to offer him such a sum… It meant the danger was very real.

Ferrara might be a billionaire, but $180,000 wasn't small change even for a billionaire.

"If I were to accept," Jordan said, staring Ferrara down, "I will need to know more than that. I'm not walking into this situation blind. So tell me more. Sir."

Over the next hour, Ferrara did tell him more. It was pretty obvious that he still left a lot unsaid, but Jordan finally had a clearer picture after putting together everything Ferrara had told him and what he could read between the lines.

There was trouble brewing among the Italian mafia. Ever since Ferrara's father, Marco Ferrara, had been murdered two months ago, there had been no new boss chosen yet, as far as Ferrara knew. Ferrara's numerous family members seemed to be fighting for the position, with several of them already dead. Ferrara was convinced that someone from his family was behind the assassination attempts on him. His clan was very traditional: usually, Ferrara would have been expected to inherit his father's criminal empire, which made him a potential risk for anyone wanting the top spot in the food chain, even though Ferrara was disowned.

"Damiano Conte," Ferrara said, pushing a photograph across his desk. "My stepbrother. Sort of."

Wondering how one became a "sort-of" stepbrother, Jordan looked at the photograph. The man in it looked a little like Ferrara: tall, fit, thick dark hair, though his face was much more angular than Ferrara's, with sharp, penetrating eyes that weren't as dark as his stepbrother's. His bespoke suit did little to hide his impressive physique, and the self-assured way he held himself made it obvious that this was a man who was used to getting his own way. A powerful man.

Tearing his gaze away, Jordan lifted his eyes to Ferrara. "Why do you suspect him?"

"Damiano is… a complicated person," Ferrara said, his expression becoming grim again. "He's the most dangerous out of them. We never had an easy relationship. As a boy he resented my position in the family, because he had to work for everything while I was born into power and money. And I used to be a total asshole, to be honest."

*Used to be?*

Jordan almost laughed. The majority of Ferrara's employees were scared shitless of him for a reason. The man was a total tyrant, and he had probably been a bully as a kid, too.

"He became more closed off and harder to read as we grew up," Ferrara said. "I haven't seen him in more than a decade. I don't know if he still hates me. He doesn't have any reason to envy me anymore—last I heard, he owns half of Italy by now. But…"

"Hatred isn't rational," Jordan said quietly. And people could hold onto childhood grudges for a long time.

Ferrara nodded. "We always competed for stuff when we were young. He liked taking things away from me. Even if he isn't behind the assassination attempts, he'll pay close attention to Nate—and I don't want Nate anywhere near him." Ferrara's expression darkened. "I may not have seen Damiano in a decade, but I've heard rumors and they're… disturbing. He's dangerous. That's the main reason why I want you to take Nate's place on this trip."

"To be a piece of meat you throw to a lion to distract him?" Jordan said wryly.

Ferrara grimaced a little but didn't even bother denying it, the asshole.

Jordan considered it for a moment.

*Could* he say no? Frankly, he doubted it, no matter what Ferrara had claimed. You didn't say no when your boss asked for help. What if Jordan said no and then Nate got hurt—or worse? Ferrara would never forgive him. He was ruthless and vindictive enough to ruin his career.

Besides, he did like Nate. He was a good guy. Jordan wanted to help him. Earning $180,000 in a week wouldn't hurt, either.

Jordan looked at his boss. "You expect me to pretend to be your boyfriend. What exactly would that entail?"

"I might touch your arm or shoulder, but other than that, there won't be any public displays of affection. There will be many old-fashioned, homophobic people in attendance, so any PDA would be considered offensive. We likely won't even be given the same room."

Inwardly, Jordan exhaled in relief. Not that Ferrara was repulsive or anything, but he didn't want to get intimate with him, or pretend to be. For one thing, Ferrara was his boss, and a man in a serious relationship. For another, Jordan was straight. Well, he had enjoyed sucking cock on occasion—during threesomes his ex-wife had talked him into—but he wasn't attracted to men at all. He had no desire to make out with Ferrara, no matter how objectively handsome he might be. Men did nothing for him, be it sexually or romantically.

"All right, I'm in," Jordan said. "When is this wedding?"

Ferrara's shoulders relaxed. "Next week."

# Chapter 2

The switch in the Fiumicino airport happened four days later. Having been in Rome for a few days already, Jordan arrived at the airport after Ferrara and Nate's plane landed and found the restroom they had agreed on beforehand.

Jordan got into a bathroom stall and glanced at his watch, trying to quash his anxiety. Hopefully he wouldn't have to wait for Nate long. He'd never been comfortable in confined spaces—that was one of the few things that rattled him, badly. Thankfully, the stalls weren't floor to ceiling, and it made him feel less claustrophobic than he otherwise would have been.

"Jordan?" someone whisper-yelled.

Thank fuck.

Jordan opened the door a crack. "Here. Get in."

He started undressing, as quickly as possible.

"I still think this is ridiculous and unnecessary," Nate muttered with a sigh, locking the door.

"Undress," Jordan said. He was already down to his boxer briefs.

Nate blushed a little, glancing at him. Unlike Jordan, he blushed easily. "This is so weird, man," he said, but complied. "You're my boss. I feel weird about wearing your clothes and you wearing mine."

Snorting, Jordan took Nate's shirt and slipped into it. They had a very similar build, with Jordan maybe being slightly more muscular. The shirt fit well, even if it wasn't as sharp as the clothes he normally wore. For a boyfriend of a billionaire, Nate dressed very low-key.

"Get dressed," Jordan said, zipping up Nate's jeans. "Leave the bathroom at least half an hour after me. Wear my sunglasses. Take my keys and my passport. The address of the apartment I've rented and my credit card are in the pocket of my shirt. Don't be shy about using my card—Ferrara will compensate me for your expenses. Wear sunglasses all the time."

"Aye-aye, boss," Nate said dryly.

"Take this phone, too," Jordan said, giving him his old cell phone. "It's already logged into my Instagram. Take some artsy pictures of Rome's sights and post them from time to time." While he wasn't much of a social media person, his family would think it strange if he went completely AWOL.

Luckily, they weren't the type of family that called each other much, preferring to text. It also helped that his parents were hosting some old friends this week and would be too busy playing golf to pay attention to what he was doing on his vacation. His sister Eloise was too busy with her brood of kids to even answer his messages. Bella was… well, she was his *ex*-wife for a reason. No one should miss him.

Still, his parents had means to track him if they wanted to.

Jordan slipped off his ring, trying not to feel guilty about it. "Wear this, too."

"Your ring?" Nate said, scrunching up his nose. "I don't think it's necessary."

"It's not just a ring," Jordan said. "It's a very sophisticated tracking device. My family owns an electronics company that produces them. They can track me through it."

Nate blinked. "Wow, and you voluntarily wear it? Isn't it a little overbearing?"

"It's something of a family tradition," Jordan said curtly. He had no intention of telling Nate that this supposed tradition started since his little brother had gone missing last year. After that, Jordan's father had insisted that everyone in the family should wear jewelry with a GPS tracker. It was invasive, sure, but Jordan knew his parents would never abuse his privacy without a very good reason, and he was willing to sacrifice some of his privacy if it made his mother sleep better.

Snapping himself out of those thoughts, Jordan raked a hand through his hair, making it as messy as Nate's. He felt underdressed in a simple T-shirt and jeans. He couldn't remember the last time he left home looking this way. "How do I look?"

"Weird," Nate said, his forehead wrinkled. "Weirdly casual and young? You do look like me."

"Perfect, then."

"There's still time to cancel the whole thing," Nate said, with something like hope in his voice.

"Not a chance," Jordan said. "I look forward to my paycheck for this. Chin up, Parrish. A week of sightseeing in Rome won't kill anyone."

Nate pulled a face, buttoning up Jordan's shirt on himself. "I know. I just… I feel useless. I'm worried something will happen to him and I won't be there."

Suppressing the urge to roll his eyes, Jordan said, "And what would you do if you were there and something did happen? Cry over him?"

Nate laughed a little. "I know. But you'd better return him safe and sound, boss." His light tone contradicted the dead serious look in his eyes. "I agreed to this only because I know he would go alone if I said no to us switching places. He can be such a stubborn son-of-a-bitch."

"He just wants you safe, Parrish."

Nate smiled humorlessly. "I know. And I love him for that, but it pisses me off, too." He rubbed the bridge of his nose, averting his gaze. "I want him to be safe, too."

Jordan sighed.

"I'll return him to you safe and sound. I give you my word." And never mind that he could give no such promise, but he saw nothing wrong with a white lie. Poor guy looked like he needed it.

Nate studied him for a moment. "You better. Go, before I change my mind."

When Jordan left the restroom and walked toward Ferrara's tall form, his boss did a double take before giving a small nod. So he did pass muster.

They got into the car, with two bodyguards getting into it after them, too. Jordan did his best to ignore them.

The drive to the estate took a little over an hour. Jordan spent it rehearsing in his head everything he knew about Nate and his relationship with Ferrara. He couldn't— wouldn't—mix anything up. He never did.

As the car finally rolled up to a big, gorgeous villa, Jordan took a deep breath.

Showtime.

As soon as they emerged out of the car, they were immediately accosted by a tall, lanky guy. He said something in Italian, his sharp brown eyes fixed on Ferrara. He barely glanced at Jordan, too busy glowering at Ferrara.

Ferrara said something back, also in Italian, looking unbothered by the hostility.

They stared each other down until the stranger finally sighed and hauled Ferrara into a hug, which Ferrara returned after a moment.

Probably one of his cousins, Jordan concluded.

He turned out to be correct when Ferrara looked at him and finally spoke in English, "This is Paolo Ferrara, my cousin. Paolo, this is Nate Parrish." He didn't offer any explanation on who "Nate" was, but a knowing gleam appeared in Paolo's eyes anyway.

Paolo gave Jordan a quick once-over and said something in Italian, smirking.

"Do you not speak English?" Jordan said, pointedly. He'd never appreciated being talked about when he didn't understand a thing.

"My apologies," Paolo said with a friendly, sheepish smile. His English was heavily accented but perfectly fine. "I said I could see why Raffa switched teams for you."

Remembering that Nate was supposed to be a friendly guy, Jordan smiled. "Thanks. Could you show us our rooms? We're pretty tired after the flight."

Paolo nodded. "Sure, let's go." He led them inside the large house. "Most of the wedding guests haven't arrived yet. It'll be only family tonight."

"Family?" Ferrara said, his face inscrutable.

Paolo shot him a look Jordan couldn't read. "Not everyone, of course. My father, *Zio* Franco, Gustavo, me and you. Andrea should arrive by the evening. The women will arrive tomorrow. They took Bianca for a bachelorette party in Milano."

"Hm," Ferrara said. "What about Damiano?"

Another strange look passed over Paolo's face.

"We don't know yet. He said he might make it to supper, but it's possible that he'll arrive only tomorrow. There's some mess with the bankers in Napoli that requires his supervision."

"Isn't Andrea responsible for Naples?" Ferrara said.

Paolo shrugged. "He is. But you know him. He's not very good at dealing with the bankers. Too blunt, no finesse. Damiano is much better at that kind of stuff." He laughed a little. "He's much better at everything."

Hmm.

Jordan kept his face bored, pretending that he wasn't paying attention to the conversation. Although Paolo masked it pretty well, there was an undercurrent of bitterness in his voice. Jordan wondered why both of the cousins seemed to dislike Damiano so much.

He would find out soon enough, he supposed.

# Chapter 3

The dinner that evening was… interesting.

There was a peculiar mix of tension, rivalry, and hostility in these people's interactions, nothing like a normal family functioned, but at the same time, they all clearly were closer than your average cousins would be.

Jordan observed the strange family dynamic, pretending to be engrossed in the food—which was delicious. He'd always been fond of Italian cuisine, so he really appreciated the chance to try authentic Italian food.

Franco and Sergio, the two elderly uncles of Ferrara, conversed exclusively in Italian and completely ignored Jordan, which would be pretty offensive if he really were Ferrara's boyfriend.

Paolo and Gustavo, as the younger generation, were polite enough to speak in English, though they often forgot themselves until Ferrara reminded them to speak in English—then they smiled sheepishly at Jordan and switched to English again. It was interesting that they both seemed to subconsciously respect Ferrara and listen to him, even though they hadn't seen him in over a decade. But then again, Raffaele Ferrara had the same effect on all his employees, and it was no wonder his cousins were no different.

Paolo was the more easygoing cousin while Gustavo was harder to read, but neither seemed capable of murdering their cousin. In fact, they seemed surprisingly normal, but then again, it was entirely possible that Jordan was allowing his preconceived ideas about the mafia to affect him, and real life was nothing like Hollywood movies.

The dinner was coming to an end when there was the sound of approaching footsteps. A man entered the dining room, and all conversations came to a halt.

"Damiano!" Sergio exclaimed before saying something in Italian.

Jordan eyed the newcomer curiously. So this was the infamous Damiano.

The photograph didn't do him justice. He was a tall man, his light blue dress shirt hugging his wide shoulders and muscular torso. His features were a little too sharp and angular to be traditionally handsome, like those of a predator, but he was a startlingly striking man. His black hair was thick and luscious, brushed back in a way only Hollywood movie stars seemed to pull off, but this man could pull off that look effortlessly. His attractiveness was undeniable; even Jordan could see it. Damiano wasn't more handsome than his cousins—Ferrara and Gustavo were more conventionally handsome—but there was something about this man that drew one's eye, something intangible.

Jordan shifted a little in his seat, which seemed to attract the man's attention to him. His gray eyes flickered over him impassively before moving to Ferrara at Jordan's right. A shade of emotion appeared in them for a moment.

"Raffaele," he said, his voice devoid of any sentiment.

"Damiano," Ferrara said, equally reserved. His hand touched Jordan's arm. "This is Nate Parrish, my partner."

Jordan simply nodded in greeting, since Ferrara wasn't bothering to get up, either.

If Damiano recognized that he wasn't actually Nate, nothing betrayed it. "A pleasure," he said, his voice smooth and low. He sat down in the empty seat opposite Jordan and a maid started serving him.

Silence reigned. There was a strange sort of weight in the air, something expectant, almost wary.

Only Damiano seemed immune to the tension, eating calmly. He wasn't oblivious to it; not at all. This man was perfectly aware of the discomfort in the room. He was *enjoying* it, Jordan realized after a moment.

At long last, Paolo broke the silence and said something in Italian. Whatever he said seemed to notch up the tension in the room even more.

Paolo's father said something, and then Ferrara spoke, his voice quiet but full of gravity.

Jordan was sick and tired of being the only person in the dark. He must have made some frustrated noise, because Damiano raised his gaze from the pasta on his fork and looked at him. His lips curled slightly, but the smile didn't touch his eyes.

"It's very impolite to speak in Italian when we have a guest who doesn't understand us," he said. A pin drop could have been heard in the silence that followed. Damiano took a sip from his red wine. "Why don't you all repeat your questions in English?"

"But…" Paolo said, glancing at Jordan hesitantly.

"He's an outsider, Damiano," Sergio said, surprising Jordan. Until now, Jordan had thought the elderly man didn't speak English.

"Isn't he Raffaele's partner?" Damiano said, looking almost bored but for the hard glint in his eyes.

"He's practically family. We can't have him feeling neglected."

Jordan wasn't sure how he felt about this man sticking up for him. He doubted Damiano cared that he felt neglected, so what was his game exactly?

"Where's Andrea?" Ferrara said. "Wasn't he supposed to arrive with you?"

All eyes fixed on Damiano, who shrugged slightly, sipping his wine. "Andrea has taken some time off to reevaluate his priorities." He looked his relatives in the eyes, one after another.

Jordan watched in surprise and reluctant admiration as every single one of them dropped their gazes—even the men twice Damiano's age. Even *Ferrara*. Jordan hadn't thought there was a man on the planet who could discomfit Raffaele-fucking-Ferrara. Apparently there was.

It made Jordan so very curious about this man. He didn't bother hiding his curiosity when Damiano's gaze stopped on him. Gray eyes met his, but Jordan refused to be intimidated. Maybe it was foolish of him, maybe he just didn't understand how dangerous this man was, but he didn't feel wary—he wasn't sure what to be wary of.

"Am I missing something or do you enjoy making your family fear you?" Jordan said, quirking his eyebrows.

The Italian smiled a little, but his eyes remained cold and unfeeling. He had very unusual eyes, the color of the ocean on a stormy day: they could look almost blue at times, and they could look very dark too.

Damiano's long, sun-bronzed fingers played with his glass idly, making the wine inside it move. "Fear me?" he said. "My family has no reason to fear me if they don't give me one. Isn't that right, Gustavo?"

Gustavo's Adam's apple bobbed. "*Si.*"

"English," Damiano said in the same soft tone that sent a chill down Jordan's spine. There was something off about this man. Something wrong.

"Y-yes, Damiano," Gustavo stammered.

Jordan was baffled—and more than a little uneasy. He was perfectly aware that all the men sitting at this table were somewhat involved in the *family business*, even Ferrara, who had grown up in such an atmosphere before moving to America. For these powerful, hardened men to be so visibly uncomfortable around their own relative… What kind of man did it take to discomfit men who were used to violence and murder?

Damiano didn't even glance at Gustavo. "See?" he said, looking at Jordan. "You will find that I value family and honesty between family members above all else."

Jordan held his gaze unflinchingly, even though it was taking all his willpower not to look away.

Did Damiano know that he wasn't Nate? It was impossible to tell. The mention of the value of honesty could be a hint that he knew—or it could be a simple coincidence and Damiano might be referring to something else entirely. The man was an enigma, his eyes unreadable and his motives impossible to discern.

It made Jordan all the more curious about him. Curiosity and a thirst for knowledge had always been both his greatest strengths and his greatest weaknesses.

He barely managed to wait until the meal was over before laying a hand on Ferrara's arm and saying loudly that he'd like to retire in a way that probably made it obvious that he was taking Ferrara away to have sex. At least from the way the older generation sneered, barely hiding their disgust, Jordan was successful at conveying that.

Paolo leered and gave them a knowing look as they left the room. Gustavo was too busy looking at something on his phone to pay attention. Jordan couldn't resist glancing back at Damiano, unsure what kind of reaction to expect. But Damiano's face was impassive, his eyes giving nothing away as he watched them go.

"Why is everyone scared of him?" Jordan said the moment he and his boss were alone in Ferrara's room.

Ferrara gave him a rather pinched look. "I'm not scared of him," he said. "But it would be stupid not to be wary of him. I know what he's capable of."

"What *is* he capable of?" Jordan said.

Ferrara sighed, loosening his tie. "Damiano is… He's always been different from the rest of us, even when we were kids."

"Isn't he your brother?" Jordan said.

"Stepbrother, and even that is a stretch," Ferrara said. "He's the son of my father's first wife."

"Really? Aren't you close in age?"

"We are."

Jordan barely swallowed a sigh of exasperation. Seriously, it was like pulling teeth. "Your father mustn't have been married to her long, then, if she had him before her marriage to your father."

Ferrara's expression became grim. "She got pregnant with Damiano while she was married to my father," he said, his tone stiff. "She was kidnapped by a Turkish mob that had a bone to pick with my father. She was raped for days. By the time she was recovered, she was already pregnant. Apparently, my father wasn't sure if the child was his or the rapist's, but the DNA test after the child's birth confirmed that it wasn't his. It destroyed their marriage. She took her life, leaving the baby in my father's care—her relatives didn't want to raise the product of their daughter's rape." His lips twisted. "Frankly, I think it also bothered them that he's mixed race. He was given their last name, against their wishes. They wanted nothing to do with their grandchild, didn't even want to see it. They were the worst sort of rich snobs, truth be told."

Jordan felt sick to his stomach. Poor kid. The child of a rapist, unwanted and abandoned by his own mother and her relatives, left in the care of the man who must have hated his very existence…

"Were?" Jordan said.

"They were shot when Damiano was sixteen. The killer was never caught."

Jordan stared at him. Surely…

"I honestly don't know," Ferrara said, shrugging. "People assume he killed them, but there's no proof. He did inherit everything they had, as their only biological grandson. Anyway, my father remarried very fast after his first wife's suicide and I was born just a year after Damiano."

"So you grew up together?"

"Sort of."

"Sort of?" Jordan said, watching dispassionately as Ferrara changed into more comfortable clothes.

"I was the heir to the clan. He was an orphan no one wanted around and who wasn't blood related to us." Ferrara sighed. "Gustavo, Andrea, Paolo and me… You know how cruel kids can be, especially privileged kids. We never really treated him like one of us. My father didn't treat him badly, but he wasn't exactly an affectionate man, either. Damiano grew up as an outsider, despite being surrounded by a large family." Ferrara rubbed his forehead, shaking his head. "As an adult, looking back, I can see where it went wrong. He was unloved and underappreciated. Lonely. He grew up with an immense thirst to prove himself, to show us that he was as good, that he was *better* than us." He smiled humorlessly. "He did prove it and then some."

Jordan frowned, trying to reconcile the lonely, unappreciated boy Ferrara was describing with the cold-eyed, unnerving man he had met, and couldn't. "What happened?"

"We all grew up," Ferrara said. "My cousins and I were privileged rich kids, so we were more complacent, assured of our place in the food chain because of who our fathers were. Damiano had no such assurance. He was single-minded in his determination to earn his place at the top, not to be a simple henchman. His ambition has always been like no one else's, and it drove him to be perfect at everything."

"Everything?" Jordan said, skeptical. No one was perfect at everything.

"Everything," Ferrara said with another humorless smile.

He sighed. "We all could handle a gun well by the time we were fifteen, but Damiano was something else. He could hit the bullseye ten times out of ten, he spoke four languages, he got perfect grades, and he could talk circles around all of us. It goes without saying that it didn't exactly make him any friends. Teenagers hate being shown up."

"You bullied him?" Jordan said quietly.

Sighing again, Ferrara rolled his shoulders. "No. At least not that I know of. He was too strong and good at hand-to-hand and with a knife to be bullied in a traditional way. But there are other ways to make a teenager feel unwanted. Lesser."

Ferrara's black eyes were solemn as he met Jordan's. "As an adult, I'm not proud of it. We were rich, cruel brats. But I can't change the past. And in our defense, we had no way of knowing that with our verbal cruelty and dismissive attitude we were creating a monster."

"A monster?" Jordan said, frowning. While Damiano had made him uneasy, he had seen nothing that indicated that he was a monster.

Ferrara walked to the window and stared out of it. "There's something broken in him," he said without any inflection. "He doesn't seem to understand what empathy is, and I'm not sure he understands that there should be a line you should never cross. He doesn't care for anything but power and mind games. Watching us squirm entertains him. A therapist would probably say he's a high-functioning sociopath—if not worse."

"With all due respect, boss, but some people in the company call *you* a sociopath," Jordan said. *Sadistic, heartless asshole,* to be precise.

A wry smile curled Ferrara's lips. "I'm aware," he said. "I would be the first to say that I'm not a nice, empathic man, but compared to Damiano, I'm the epitome of empathy. For Damiano people are just chess pieces he moves around to get the outcome he wants. He doesn't see them as individuals. He doesn't care for a single person. I'm not sure he's capable of it." He met Jordan's eyes. "He's the type of person who can casually pull out a gun and shoot all of us at the table and then go back to his dinner."

Jordan stared at him. Was he serious?

"He's trigger-happy?"

"No," Ferrara said with a grimace. "He would do it in cold blood. Damiano doesn't do anything without a good reason, but the way his mind works isn't normal. *He* isn't normal. Be very careful around him. He's paying you even more attention than I expected. I don't like the way he looks at you. Be careful."

"I will," Jordan said and left the room, feeling more alarmed than he had been in a long time.

And so very curious.

# Chapter 4

Jordan tossed and turned in bed, unable to sleep. Partly it was anxiety, but mostly it was his curiosity. Ferrara's explanation hadn't satisfied it. He had so many questions now, his brain unable to turn off.

Around midnight, he gave up and got out of the bed.

The house was quiet and dark. The windows were wide open, bringing the sweet smell of flowers from the garden. Jordan padded toward the terrace he'd glimpsed upon their arrival and pushed the door open.

He stepped out and breathed in deeply, leaning against the wall. There was something about the scent of Italian air that made him want to stay outside and stargaze. Maybe he just missed being in the countryside. He'd barely left Boston in a decade, and when he did, it was always for work.

A sound snapped him out of his thoughts. Frowning, Jordan looked toward it before slowly heading in that direction. He rounded the house and saw a large pool. It was well lit despite the hour—and there was someone there.

A man was swimming in it with strong, sure strokes, cleaving through the water until he flipped over onto his back. The lights illuminated his broad, sun-bronzed shoulders and muscular chest, angular face and black hair.

Jordan's stomach clenched.

He took a step back behind the thick oak, not wanting to be seen, not wanting to be caught spying. But he couldn't make himself leave completely. He watched Damiano float in the water, his big body relaxed like that of a panther.

Now that he knew what to look for, Jordan could see what Ferrara meant about Damiano not being fully Italian. Something about his eyes, the harsh curve of his dark eyebrows, and his strong facial structure reminded him of those ruthless Ottoman sultans from the Turkish TV series that his mother liked watching so much. It gave Damiano's face such strength and character, made it more striking than Ferrara's more conventionally handsome face was.

He wondered how this man felt about seeing his nameless father's features on his own face. Did he hate it? Or did he not care at all?

Jordan tried to quash his curiosity. Curiosity could be very dangerous when it came to this man, if Ferrara was correct about him.

The sound of footsteps made him wrench his gaze from Damiano. A woman came into view. All she had on her was a short, half-sheer black robe, her long red hair nearly reaching her barely covered ass. She said something in Italian, her tone unmistakably flirtatious.

Damiano opened his eyes and looked at her impassively. He said something, his deep voice not betraying the content of his words at all. He certainly didn't sound like he was flirting back.

But the woman smiled and, throwing her robe off, sauntered into the pool, completely naked.

Jordan certainly appreciated the view, but he found his gaze inexplicably drawn back to Damiano. Something about this man was like the gravitational pull of a black hole: it was so difficult to tear one's gaze from him. His sheer *presence* was incredible, strong enough to distract a man from the sight of a naked, gorgeous woman.

Damiano moved to the shallow end of the pool and leaned back against the stairs, still half-submerged in the water. When the woman knelt in front of him and kissed his muscular stomach, nuzzling the dark trail of hair leading downward to a big, half-hard cock, Jordan told himself to look away. He told himself to get the hell out of there. He'd never been a voyeur.

But his feet didn't seem to listen to the commands of his brain at all. He watched, transfixed, as Damiano's face became tenser, his muscles flexing and stiffening as the woman pleasured him. If Jordan didn't know better, he'd think she was causing him pain—he was so rigid and weirdly still, his face betraying none of the pleasure he ought to be feeling.

Jordan tried to look away, very much aware that it was creepy to stare at a man while someone sucked that man's cock. But he couldn't.

The woman made a sound, and Jordan finally wrenched his gaze away to look at her. She was moaning around the cock in her mouth, choking on it as she struggled to take it all. She pulled up for breath, revealing the thick, long cock in her hand, glistening at the fat tip. It was very veiny. Obscenely big, like something from porn.

Jordan moistened his lips.

He blamed his reluctant fascination with cocks on Bella for all the threesomes she had talked him into while they had been married. He hadn't had a cock in his mouth since before their divorce. He might have liked sucking cock on occasion, but he was hardly going to go looking for one. He wasn't gay.

The woman swallowed the cock again, and Jordan returned his gaze to Damiano's face.

He found him looking straight at him.

Jordan froze.

And then he turned, and all but ran away.

His heart pounding, he returned to his room and leaned heavily against the door, his breath coming in short gasps.

He crawled into his bed, the sheets cool against his overheated skin.

Fuck.

Maybe once he returned home, he *should* go looking for a cock to suck, if he got so worked up from just looking at that creep's cock.

It had been a really nice cock, though.

Jordan scowled and, yanking his shorts down, jerked off, without thinking about anything in particular. He just wanted release. He was wound up too tightly. It was fast and rough, and his orgasm was unsatisfying, barely enough to take the edge off, the tension under his skin still there. It was frustrating as hell; Jordan felt like punching someone.

After a few more hours of tossing and turning, he managed to fall asleep.

His dreams were strange.

*Skin. So much skin. It was that gorgeous redhead that he'd seen with Damiano. Her full breasts bounced enticingly as she was fucked hard, tan male hands bruising her hips and holding her legs spread. A cock pistoned in and out of her, thick, long, and veiny. She was moaning continuously, as if that cock was the best thing she'd ever felt. Gray eyes glared down at her—him?—and Jordan shivered and reached up, grabbing the muscular shoulders as—*

*The dream changed.*

*Jordan was kneeling on the dirty floor of a stall in a public bathroom. He was sucking on the fat cock peeking out of the hole in the wall. A glory hole. He was sucking cock at a glory hole. He was moaning around the thick shaft, enjoying how good it felt in his mouth. Just some anonymous, no-strings-attached fun. He didn't care who the cock belonged to. All he wanted was this cock. This thick, delicious cock.*

*But then the wall between the stalls disappeared and there were hands on his head, strong and hard, yanking him down onto that cock, fucking him brutally, forcing him to take it. Gagging, Jordan looked up.*

*Gray eyes locked with his.*

Jordan sat up in the bed, panting, and stared at his wet boxers in confusion. Had he really just come in his sleep? That hadn't happened to him since he was a teenager. He couldn't even remember what he had been dreaming about—just a vague impression of skin and want.

Bizarre.

Shrugging it off, Jordan kicked off his boxers, turned onto his stomach and fell asleep again.

# Chapter 5

Jordan woke up feeling cranky and tired. He went to the ensuite and stared in the mirror at his dry skin and bloodshot eyes. This wouldn't do. He was supposed to be a guy in his twenties, and guys in their twenties didn't look like this after a bad night's sleep.

A warm shower and his skin moisturizer helped him feel human again. He would have felt even better if he could've used his hair gel and worn his normal clothes instead of the T-shirts and jeans Nate wore, but he could put up with Nate's lack of style for a week, since he was getting paid handsomely for it. It would be the easiest $180,000 he'd ever made.

Piercing gray eyes flashed to the forefront of his mind, but Jordan shoved the thought away. He wasn't afraid of the man, no matter how interesting and dangerous that man was. So what if Damiano had seen him last night? Watching a man receive head wasn't a crime—creepy and somewhat embarrassing, yes, but hardly suspicious. Damiano had probably already forgotten about it; Jordan should do the same. He would keep a low profile for a week, help Ferrara find out who was targeting him if possible, and then receive his paycheck. Easy.

Feeling calmer, Jordan got dressed in a blue T-shirt that flattered his eyes and complexion before slipping into a pair of jeans, and went downstairs.

The house was loud this morning.

It confused Jordan a little, since the wedding wasn't until tomorrow, before he remembered that the ladies of the family were supposed to arrive from Milan.

Putting on his friendliest expression, he headed toward the sound of voices—toward the living room.

Ferrara was seated in the big armchair by the open windows and he had two little girls in his lap. He was surrounded by a gaggle of smiling women, talking to him animatedly in Italian.

Jordan stared at his normally formidable, unapproachable boss, wondering if he'd woken up in an alternate reality.

The side of his face prickled with awareness, and Jordan stiffened, feeling someone's eyes on him.

He turned his head and found Damiano lounging on the couch in the far corner of the room, as far from Ferrara and the women as it was possible to be.

Damiano's eyes met his, and Jordan hoped he wasn't blushing. He wasn't really the blushing type, but his face suddenly felt uncomfortably warm as he remembered last night.

Damiano tilted his head slightly and looked at the seat beside him. A silent command to come to him.

Jordan considered refusing or pretending not to understand. He was more than a little miffed, truth be told. He wasn't some—some *underling* to be ordered around. But his curiosity won out.

He headed toward Damiano and took the seat beside him with an air of nonchalance, as if he weren't acutely aware of the man next to him. "Hi," he said. "Lovely morning, isn't it?"

Damiano regarded him for a moment. "Why didn't you sleep in Raffaele's room?"

All right. Apparently, they weren't doing small talk.

Jordan raised his eyebrows and put on a mildly amused look. "I'm surprised you found time between fucking that redhead and fucking with your family to spy on our sleeping arrangements." There. If he mentioned last night's incident himself, Damiano wouldn't be able to hold it over his head.

"What makes you think I'm fucking with my family?"

Jordan smiled. "Please. Last evening you were getting a kick out of having them all quake in their boots. What did you do to Andrea to make them so scared?"

The bored look was gone from Damiano's eyes. Now there was something like curiosity in them as he studied Jordan, as if he were a lowlife far beneath his notice that had just done some unexpected trick.

"Why didn't you ask your sugar daddy?" Damiano said, his lips curling in derision.

Had Nate been here right now, he would have probably exploded with indignation and denial. But frankly, Jordan didn't really disagree with Damiano: the power imbalance and financial gap between Ferrara and Nate was so vast, it wasn't inaccurate to call Ferrara Nate's sugar daddy, even if their relationship dynamic was different.

Of course, the term wouldn't apply to Jordan if he really were Ferrara's boyfriend. While he might not be a billionaire, he came from an old, wealthy family and he did pretty well for himself.

Not to mention that he was hardly sugar baby material: he was a grown man close to Ferrara and Damiano's ages.

"We had better things to do last evening than gossip about you," Jordan said. He wasn't trying to be subtle at all: he needed to erase any suspicion caused by their sleeping arrangements, and Nate wasn't really a subtle guy.

Damiano stared at him in a way that made Jordan feel uncomfortably transparent. He suddenly remembered Ferrara's words—his astounding claim that this man was perfect at everything. Even if it was an exaggeration, there was little doubt how intelligent Damiano had to be to excel at most things. This was a very smart man. Not an easily fooled one.

"Andrea attempted to kill me," Damiano said in a low voice, actually answering his question, to Jordan's astonishment. "He's been taught a lesson."

It was Jordan's turn to stare. "You let him live after he attempted to kill you?" He barely knew this man, but showing mercy seemed uncharacteristic for him, considering everything Ferrara had told him. "Why?"

Damiano cocked his head, studying him. "Why do you think?"

Rubbing his chin and lips in thought, Jordan looked down.

He hated that a part of him wanted to get the answer right, to show off for this man, to make him respect him. It was utterly revolting. He didn't need this man's respect.

"Killing him would have been easy," he said slowly, looking up to watch Damiano's reaction. "You don't really think of him as a threat. By letting him live you can have him followed and can find out who his co-conspirators are."

Damiano's expression didn't change. "You're not incorrect," he said at last. "But that's not the only reason I let him live."

Jordan let out a fake yawn and looked away, hoping he looked disinterested. He'd be damned if he let this arrogant man see that he was burning with curiosity. *Come on, tell me, tell me, tell me.*

Damiano chuckled. "You're positively adorable."

Maybe he'd misheard.

"Pardon?" Jordan said, without looking at him. It took everything in him not to look at him.

He felt the other man lean closer to him and then murmur close to his ear, "It's adorable how you pretend not to be interested when spying on me is the main reason you're here."

Jordan's heart jumped into his throat, or at least attempted to. "I don't know what you're talking about," he managed with a dry mouth, still not looking at him.

"Let's cut the bullshit," Damiano said, his voice still soft and nice. "I know Raffaele. I know how possessive of his things he is. He would never let us speak alone like this if he didn't bring you here with an ulterior motive."

Inwardly, Jordan breathed out. So Damiano didn't know that he wasn't Nate. Sure, it wasn't ideal that he suspected him, but at least he didn't suspect that he was the wrong guy. He could work with that.

Jordan turned his head and nearly flinched as he ended up nose to nose with Damiano. "All right, fine," he said, refusing to be the one to pull away, no matter how much this man unnerved him. He wasn't going to be intimidated that easily, damn it. "You're right: Raffaele told me to keep my guard up around you. To keep an eye on you. He doesn't trust you. But that doesn't make me a spy.

That's ridiculous."

"Is it?" Damiano murmured, holding his gaze unblinkingly. Like a snake.

Jesus, it was incredibly hard to keep eye contact with this man, especially when their faces were less than two inches apart.

"Yes," Jordan said belatedly, unsure what he was even replying to. He'd lost track of the conversation, his thoughts scattering, his heart beating fast and his palms sweaty. He'd never been so unnerved by a man.

*Just a man*, he told himself.

*A high-functioning sociopath*, Ferrara's voice said in his head.

"Sure," Damiano said dryly, *finally* pulling back a little and allowing him to breathe. "You can report to Raffaele that I didn't kill Andrea because of Emma."

"Emma?" Jordan repeated, watching Damiano pull out a cigarette and light it.

Firm lips curled around the cigarette. "Andrea's wife. Real beauty, but she looks dreadful in black."

Jordan laughed a little. "Right. I'm sure that's the reason you didn't kill him. And don't smoke indoors."

Damiano shrugged, taking another drag of his cigarette. "Believe what you want. I don't care. But tell Raffaele he can ask me questions himself instead of making his sugar baby make doe eyes at me."

"Fuck you," Jordan said. Doe eyes? He never fucking made doe eyes, much less at this creep. But on the bright side, that proved that he was convincing enough as Nate—it proved that he had this arrogant dick utterly fooled.

Chuckling, Damiano got to his feet and patted him on the head condescendingly, like one would pat a *dog*. "You're pretty enough, for a guy, but I don't swing that way, so your doe eyes are wasted on me, *bello*."

That pissed Jordan off enough to get to his feet, too, and give him his sweetest smile. "Neither did Raffaele, and yet." Raffaele Ferrara had been straight as an arrow until Nate; everyone knew it.

Damiano paused and gave him a considering look. "That's true," he said, looking almost… intrigued. He gave Jordan a scrutinizing look from head to toe. Jordan felt like a strange specimen in a zoo.

"Stop smoking in my face," he said bitingly, trying to hide his discomfort. Jordan had never had low self-esteem. He knew he was handsome, the type of handsome that made people do a double take and turn back to look at him when he passed them. He looked a lot younger than his thirty-two years, his skin smooth and nearly flawless, no visible wrinkles thanks to his skincare routine. Frankly, he was more handsome than Nate.

But right now, under this man's scrutiny, he felt about as ugly as the proverbial duckling. He'd never felt so self-conscious about his looks in his life.

"You're different from what I expected," Damiano said at last, removing the cigarette from his lips.

Jordan's heart skipped a beat. "In what way?"

The other man glanced at Ferrara before looking back at him. "A lot less meek. Raffaele is the type of self-centered asshole who doesn't tolerate back-talk—I'm surprised he puts up with you."

"You haven't seen him in a decade. How do you know what he's like now?"

Damiano let out a soft snort. "People don't really change. Or rather, 'nice' people can change for the worse, but assholes? Never."

"You're very cynical," Jordan said, roaming his gaze

over that hard, emotionless face. It repelled him as much as it fascinated him.

"Just pragmatic," Damiano said, shrugging. "Everyone has the capacity to be an asshole, given the right incentive, but assholes never become nice guys, not truly. Or are you under a delusion that Raffaele is a nice man?"

Jordan nearly laughed. "I know he isn't," he said, choosing his words carefully and trying to adopt the soft, smitten expression he'd seen on Nate's face when he spoke of Ferrara. "But I don't need him to be a nice guy to love him."

Something shifted in Damiano's eyes. "Oh, really?" he said with a twisted sneer on his lips. "Are you actually claiming to love him?"

Lifting his chin, Jordan held his gaze. "Yes. So what?"

Damiano laughed, white teeth flashing against his tan skin. He leaned in and said into Jordan's ear, his voice a low, intimate murmur, "If you really loved him, you wouldn't look at me like you want to choke on my cock."

Jordan spluttered in indignation, but before he could say anything, Damiano walked out of the room.

# Chapter 6

Jordan normally wasn't easily ruffled. In fact, most people working under him thought he was cold and emotionless—he'd actually overheard his subordinates call him an emotionless asshole with a stick up his ass. It was an image Jordan had cultivated himself. It was an image he was proud of.

But right now he was as far from emotionless as he could get. He *seethed* every time he looked at Damiano during lunch. Luckily, they were seated pretty far from each other, or Jordan probably wouldn't have been able to eat at all. His appetite was gone every time he glanced toward the end of the table—at the *head* of the table. Why was that dick seated at the head of the table, exactly? It was absolutely sickening the way everyone bent over backward trying not to piss him off. Even Ferrara, who normally had an ego big enough for two, was quiet and wary as he watched his stepbrother with unreadable dark eyes.

It was a small consolation that at least no one seemed to like the asshole. They respected Damiano, most of them clearly feared him, but there wasn't a single person in the room who looked at him kindly. If Damiano hadn't been such a self-important ass, Jordan would have felt sorry for him. But as things stood, he totally understood why no one liked him. Who would like that presumptuous, arrogant—

"If you keep staring at Damiano, Raffaele might get the wrong idea."

Yanking his gaze away, Jordan shifted it to the petite young woman seated to his right: Lucrezia, Ferrara's younger cousin.

Lucrezia was smiling crookedly, the way people smiled when they weren't sure what to think.

"I wasn't staring," Jordan said, grabbing his coffee. It was cold. He had been distracted.

Her expression skeptical, Lucrezia raised her fine dark eyebrows. "Between you and me," she murmured just for Jordan's ears. "I used to stare at Damiano, too, when I was a teenager—he isn't actually blood-related to me, you know." She winced, looking a little embarrassed. "He was deliciously forbidden: a relative but not, with a tragic backstory and dashing good looks." She snorted. "I was a stupid little girl. I know better now."

"What do you mean?" Jordan said, against his better judgment. He sipped his cold coffee just to appear nonchalant.

"Damiano is…" Her expression became somber before she shook her head and smiled. "He's so out of my league it isn't even funny. If only you saw the women who keep his company… Drop-dead gorgeous, every single one of them."

Jordan had a feeling it wasn't what she had intended to say, but he pretended to believe her, despite his burning curiosity.

His gaze returned to the man in question, but he quickly looked away when he realized that Lucrezia was still watching him. He hadn't been staring, damn it.

Jordan stabbed the salad on his plate with his fork. "So is the fight for the top dog position over?"

He murmured, "Everyone seems to have bared their bellies and submitted to him like a bitch."

Lucrezia snickered. "I like English expressions — they're so funny." She sipped her tea and shrugged with one delicate shoulder. "It does seem to be unofficially over. Uncle Andrea was the last one who was still trying to go head to head with Damiano, but well… I guess now it's over. Frankly, the only one who stood a chance to go against Damiano was always Raffaele. He certainly has the strength of character, intelligence, and balls, and he's the blood heir, but he's such an *American* these days." She said the word as if it were something uncomplimentary. Maybe it was. "If he were interested, things would have gotten… a lot more interesting, let's just say, but Raffaele has made himself pretty clear that he has no interest in returning to Italy and taking over the family business."

"So the king is dead, long live the king — just like that?" Jordan said. "Even though most people at the table hate Damiano's guts?"

Lucrezia gave a small, twisted smile. "Damiano doesn't want our acceptance or love, Nate. He's respected, feared, and obeyed — that's all he wants. He isn't one for sentiment. He doesn't have a sentimental bone in his body."

Jordan frowned. Lucrezia's words confirmed Ferrara's, but they were still hard to believe. It was human nature to crave social acceptance and affection. How could a normal human being survive without an ounce of affection or positive feeling in his life?

But if Damiano really was a sociopath, he might not even understand affection.

"I saw him with a woman last night," Jordan said. "But she isn't here. Does he have a girlfriend?"

Lucrezia snickered. "A girlfriend? I don't think that word is in his vocabulary. He rarely sleeps with the same woman twice. She's probably gone already—they don't spend the night. He doesn't sleep when there are other people in the room."

"He's that paranoid?"

Lucrezia shrugged. "I think the paranoia is justified, considering that people have been attempting to kill him in his sleep since he was a teen. Once it became obvious how high the 'bastardo' was aiming, that pissed off a lot of people. But he survived, and the adversity only made him stronger."

Jordan felt a pang of sadness. Jesus. Trying to assassinate a teenager in his sleep... He could only imagine how that would affect a kid during his formative years.

Jordan looked back at the cold-eyed man at the head of the table, not sure what to feel.

"*Zio* Damiano!" a childish voice exclaimed before a very short person climbed into Damiano's lap. The chubby little girl, no older than four or five, pecked Damiano loudly on his cheek, giving him a sweet smile and chattering nonstop in Italian.

"What?" Jordan whispered, staring at the strange sight. Damiano wasn't smiling at the girl—his expression was faintly long-suffering and irritated—but he was tolerating having a very loud child on his lap with surprising patience.

Lucrezia snorted softly. "Sofia is about the only person in the family that has no fear of Damiano. She likes him."

"Who is she?"

"She's Andrea's daughter. They must have arrived at last."

Jordan frowned, looking from Damiano's irritated expression to the little girl's adoring face. She didn't seem bothered by his visible displeasure.

Oh.

Before he could fully formulate the thought, there was the sound of adult voices and a man and a woman entered the room.

A strange sort of tension filled the room, all conversations coming to a halt.

Jordan could deduce that the man with an appallingly bruised face was the Andrea person he'd heard so much about. The guy who had tried to kill Damiano—and had been "taught a lesson." Judging by the careful way he moved, the lesson must have been very thorough. He seemed to have a broken rib or two, but he was putting on a brave face, greeting his relatives with a small smile.

A smile none of them returned, watching for Damiano's reaction.

"Sofia," Andrea said at last, looking at his daughter and avoiding the eyes of the man she was seated in the lap of. "Don't bother Damiano."

It confused Jordan why he wasn't speaking in Italian, before realizing that one of his relatives must have informed him of Damiano's order to speak English, and Andrea was trying hard not to piss him off.

Christ. Talk about rolling over and showing one's belly.

Damiano studied Andrea for a long, charged moment, his expression impassive, before saying, "I'm glad you made it. Bianca would have been upset if you missed her wedding. Sit."

Andrea and the woman, presumably his wife Emma, sat down hurriedly, strained smiles on their lips.

And then everyone resumed talking, as if people at this table hadn't tortured or attempted to murder each other just yesterday.

Jesus, this family was so dysfunctional.

# Chapter 7

"So is it over?" Jordan asked Ferrara that evening.

They were playing chess in Ferrara's room, to give the appearance that they had retired for some quality alone time. After Damiano's comment, Jordan burned to prove him wrong and appear the most besotted boyfriend in the world, who very much *wasn't* gagging for Damiano's cock. He wasn't even thinking about that asshole.

"What do you mean?" Ferrara said, rather distractedly, as he looked at his phone. Jordan would bet all his money he was texting Nate: only Nate seemed to make Ferrara's eyes soften in such a way.

"Damiano won, didn't he? Is it over, then? The assassination attempts on you?"

Ferrara's dark brows drew together. He set his phone aside and eyed the chessboard between them. "I don't know. I can sense that something is off."

"What do you mean?"

Shrugging, Ferrara rubbed between his brows with his fingers. "It's been years since I interacted with my family, but I still know them well enough to sense that it's not over. Something is about to happen."

A sense of foreboding appeared in Jordan's insides. "When?"

Ferrara's black eyes met his. "Soon."

***

The wedding day was cloudless, sunny, and beautiful.

But Jordan barely had time to notice that.

He had *overslept*.

It had never happened to him; he'd always been punctual to a fault. But Ferrara's admonishment had made him anxious enough that he fell asleep close to dawn—and overslept.

The wedding was supposed to start at eleven in the morning in Rome. It was almost ten already, and Rome was an hour's drive away.

Jordan dressed as fast as he could and hurried downstairs.

As he had expected, everyone seemed to be gone already.

No, not everyone: there was still a car pulling away.

Jordan ran after it, waving his arms like a madman. "Wait!"

The car lurched to a halt, and the back door opened.

"Thanks!" Jordan said, panting as he jumped into it. "I overslept—" He cut himself off upon seeing the other occupant of the car.

Damiano raised his eyebrows, nursing what looked like a cup of coffee. "You're lucky my car had a flat tire, or you would have missed the wedding. I'm surprised Raffaele left you behind."

Jordan glared at him. "He probably decided that I needed my sleep after I barely slept last night. He wore me out." He knew saying that was utterly unnecessary, but he couldn't resist rubbing in that arrogant asshole's face all the amazing sex he and Ferrara were supposedly having.

Cocking his head slightly, Damiano stared at him for a moment before looking out the window at the passing scenery.

Jordan turned to his own window, too, but after a few moments, his gaze gravitated back to Damiano.

The asshole looked unfairly good in a tux. Then again, the "tall, dark, and handsome" type usually did. Still, the guy could have put some effort into his appearance. He could have at least shaved. The dark stubble on Damiano's lean cheek looked prickly to the touch.

A dimple appeared in said cheek as Damiano smiled wryly. "Are you sure he wore you out? You seem pretty thirsty to me."

"I'm surprised you managed to get into the car with a head that big. Don't flatter yourself. I'm not gay."

Gray eyes looked at him with something like detached amusement. "Unless Raffaele changed his gender when he moved to America, he's in possession of a cock and balls."

"He's the sole exception," Jordan said, kicking himself mentally for his slip. Thankfully, if he remembered correctly, Nate really hadn't had relationships with men before Ferrara.

"Is he?" Damiano said, leaning back against the rich brown leather cushion of his seat in that quintessential, relaxed alpha-male pose, his legs slightly apart to accommodate his cock and balls—not that Jordan was thinking about this man's cock and balls.

He mirrored Damiano's pose and stared him down. "Yes."

Damiano's lips curled. "I don't think—"

Gunshots pierced the air, and the tires screeched as

the car spun and came to a halt.

Instinctively, Jordan ducked, grabbing the front seat for support. His heart pounding, he looked at the other man.

All amusement had left Damiano's face, his eyes hard and focused. "Stay down," he ordered, opening a compartment under the passenger seat and retrieving a gun and bullets. He said something in Italian to the driver, but he didn't respond.

When Jordan cautiously looked at the driver's seat, he felt bile rise to his throat when he saw blood. Lots and lots of blood.

The man was dead.

Their driver was dead. Just like that.

Shaking his shock off, Jordan turned his head, but Damiano was already outside the car. Gunshots rained around. How many hostiles were there, exactly?

Cautiously, Jordan peeked out the window and paled when he saw three black vans, each containing at least eight gunmen in black masks.

Where the fuck were Damiano's bodyguards?

Jordan looked back and saw an overturned, burning car in the distance. Looked like that was the answer to his question. They were on their own.

Considering how badly they were outnumbered, he was surprised they were still alive. But then he looked at Damiano—and stared.

Apparently Ferrara hadn't been exaggerating when he said Damiano could hit the bullseye ten times out of ten. Jordan could only stare with a slack jaw as Damiano methodically shot down their would-be assassins one after another. He didn't waste bullets, his aim as precise as that of a machine.

Each shot hit its target with incredible accuracy and speed, and their attackers' numbers were dwindling. They were hesitating, probably perfectly aware of Damiano's reputation and skill with the gun.

But that wouldn't be enough. One man, no matter how good, could never out-shoot two dozen men forever. They'd overwhelm him soon enough.

Jordan reached into the compartment Damiano had gotten his gun from, and was relieved to find another gun there.

The model was unfamiliar to him, but its weight was still comforting in his hand. Taking off the safety, Jordan ducked out of the car. Crouching behind it, he aimed and took a shot. The first bullet went wide, but his second hit the mark: a man in a black mask made a gurgling sound and fell to the ground, blood pouring from the wound in his belly.

Swallowing, Jordan pushed it to the back of his mind. Later. He didn't have time to dwell on it. He didn't have time to freak out.

His hand didn't shake as he found another target and pulled the trigger. Miss. Miss. Hit. Miss. Hit. Miss. Hit. He missed more than he hit the—the *targets*, but he distracted their attackers enough not to allow them all to focus on Damiano and overwhelm him.

When he ran out of bullets, Jordan ducked behind the car again and shifted his gaze to Damiano, trying hard not to think about the fact that he'd just taken life. Four lives. Nausea churned in his gut.

It was a good thing Damiano was an excellent distraction. He truly was mesmerizing to watch. He shot men, picked up their guns, and used them, always in motion as bullets rained down on him, yet somehow he was still alive. If killing so many men bothered him, he didn't show it, his gaze focused and laser-sharp as he shot one man after another, gray eyes cold and assessing. Cool-headed. Totally in control.

Jordan watched him, transfixed, unable to look away. He always appreciated competence, and this was so far beyond competence it was impossible to avert his gaze.

That was why he noticed too late the gaseous substance in the air. His thoughts started clouding, becoming slower, his eyelids growing incredibly heavy and his body weak. The next thing he knew, everything was black.

# Chapter 8

He regained consciousness slowly.

The first thing he became aware of was the cold. He was so cold that he was actually shivering.

It baffled him enough to force him to open his eyes. He was sprawled on his back on something hard. The ceiling he was staring at looked like… rock?

Forcing the grogginess away, Jordan hauled himself into a sitting position and looked around. He was in a tiny room, maybe forty-six square feet at most. The walls were an odd mix of man-made and natural, as if it was a room that was built in a cave. The air was very moist, and the humidity made the chill even more unpleasant than it otherwise would have been. It was dark, wherever he was, a dim, old-fashioned lamp up high on the wall the only source of light. There was a dirty toilet in the corner.

There were no windows and no visible doors.

Feeling a jolt of panic, Jordan looked around, searching for the door frantically. It had to be there. He couldn't have fucking been teleported here. There was no reason to panic.

Unfortunately, his claustrophobia couldn't be rationalized away. His heart hammering in his chest, he staggered to his feet. Door. He needed to find the damn door.

He stumbled against something and nearly fell.

Squinting in the poor light, Jordan looked down.

Oh. He wasn't sure how he'd missed a body on the floor.

It was Damiano. He was lying on his stomach, very still.

He… he wasn't dead, was he?

Holding his breath, Jordan turned him onto his back and breathed out when he saw his chest rise and fall. Not dead, then. He'd probably been knocked out by the same gas. Jordan couldn't see any visible wounds, though it was hard to tell in the semi-darkness.

Sighing, Jordan searched his pockets for his phone and wasn't surprised not to find it. Their kidnappers would have been extremely incompetent if they didn't bother taking their phones. Damiano's pockets were empty too.

Leaving him be, Jordan straightened up again. Having another person with him, even if that person was Damiano, calmed him down a little—not enough to completely eradicate his claustrophobia, but enough to make his heartbeat slightly steadier as he continued the search.

He didn't find the door. He found a hatch in the ceiling.

Jordan stared at it in puzzlement before realizing that they must be in some kind of basement. That explained the humidity and the faint smell of potatoes, as if this place had been a root cellar before being repurposed.

He was in a tiny cellar. Deep underground.

Another wave of panic hit him, making it hard to breathe. Jordan hastily returned to Damiano's side and grabbed his lax hand. Finding his pulse, Jordan focused on it and breathed. He wasn't alone. It would be fine.

He needed to calm the fuck down.

He was a grown man, not a kid anymore. Fearing enclosed spaces was irrational. Illogical.

"Why are you attempting to crush my hand?"

Jordan nearly jumped. He snatched his hand away and curled it in his lap. "I was checking your pulse."

Damiano sat up. The cellar wasn't well lit enough to read his expression well, but his eyes settled on Jordan after sweeping a quick look at their surroundings. He looked remarkably calm for someone locked up in an unidentified place after fighting for his life.

"You're trembling," Damiano remarked. He didn't sound the least bit sympathetic or concerned; it was just an objective statement.

"I'm cold," Jordan said, which was true enough, even if it wasn't the only reason for his discomfort. The temperature couldn't possibly be higher than five degrees above freezing. The fabric of his tux was rather thin, suitable for hot Italian summers, not for cold root cellars with high humidity. He felt miserably cold.

Damiano studied him for a few moments. "You and Raffaele weren't aware of the attack."

"What clued you in?" Jordan said, trying to sound snide but probably failing. Fuck, he felt like the walls were closing in on him.

"Raffaele wouldn't allow his precious boyfriend's life to be in danger. He would have told you if he knew and you wouldn't have been in my car."

Now probably wasn't a good time to confess that he wasn't actually Ferrara's boyfriend and Ferrara didn't give two shits about him.

Jordan felt uneasy as it suddenly occurred to him that this might be the real reason why Ferrara made him take Nate's place: he knew what was coming and didn't want

Nate to be caught in the crossfire.

No. He was being ridiculous. Raffaele Ferrara was an asshole, but he wouldn't intentionally do it to him if he knew what was coming. Besides, what were the odds of Jordan oversleeping and catching a ride in Damiano's car?

*But that might be precisely why Ferrara didn't wake you up,* the Devil's advocate said in his mind. *He might have known about the attack on Damiano and wanted you to stay safe at the villa. Out of the way.*

That was… possible.

"You killed four of our attackers," Damiano said, as if speaking about the weather. "You're a pretty good shot."

Jordan's stomach churned at the reminder. He'd been good at pushing the thought to the back of his mind. But he had taken life. Four lives. Those men might have been attempting to kill them, but they were still men who probably had families. Spouses. Children.

He swallowed, squeezing his eyes shut. One more thing to feel shitty about.

"That's the last thing I needed to be reminded about right now," he said dryly. "It's like you're praising me on my cooking skills."

"There's a difference? A skill is a skill."

Jordan snorted, but he couldn't deny that talking to Damiano helped. It was a wonderful distraction from the fact that they were in a tiny cellar. Damiano had a really good voice: low-pitched and pleasant without being too gruff. He would have made a great audiobook narrator—if he had any emotional range.

"How many did you kill?" Jordan said, breathing deeply, in and out.

He was calm. They weren't going to run out of air. Everything was fine.

"I don't keep count. What's wrong with you?" Damiano said in a somewhat baffled, demanding tone.

"I hate confined spaces," Jordan said, tugging his knees to his chest and hugging them tightly. "The fact that we're underground doesn't help, either. It feels too much like—like a…"

"Like a tomb."

"Yep," Jordan said, grimacing. Distraction. He needed a distraction. "Who do you think is behind this?"

Damiano was quiet for a while.

"That was an inside job," he said at last. "The flat tire was no coincidence. So someone with access to my car. Someone from the family."

Ouch.

Silence fell again.

"Are you really surprised?" Jordan said. "You can't rule with fear."

"I can, but no, I'm not surprised."

"What do you mean?" Jordan said, opening his eyes and looking at the other man.

Damiano's gaze was hooded.

Unreadable.

"Doesn't matter."

Jordan frowned as a thought suddenly occurred to him. Could their kidnapper be the same person who had tried to kidnap Nate? "You aren't the one who targeted me and Raffaele."

"Of course not," Damiano said, scoffing. "I know Raffaele isn't interested in taking his father's place. If he were, he and Marco wouldn't have gone to great pains to pretend that Marco disowned him and cut off all ties to him. Raffaele isn't even in Marco's will."

Huh.

Jordan searched Damiano's face, but he seemed honest enough. And he didn't think Damiano would bother lying when they both were kidnapped and their prospects of escaping looked rather bleak.

"Why do you think we're still alive?" he said, focusing his eyes on Damiano's face and trying to trick his mind into believing that they weren't in a small box deep underground.

For the first time, he was grateful for the gravitational black hole Damiano was: it was easy to keep his eyes on him and forget about the walls around them. Damiano's angular, sharp face looked even more predatory and interesting to watch in the dim yellow light: like something from an old painting.

Seemingly deep in thought, Damiano yanked at his bow tie and threw it aside. "It's not ransom they're after," he said, unbuttoning the top button of his shirt. "No one will pay ransom for me."

The saddest part was how matter-of-fact Damiano was about it.

"They probably do intend to make Raffaele pay ransom for you," Damiano said after a moment. "But me..." He smiled wryly, rubbing at his stubbled jaw. "I foresee some old-fashioned torture in my near future. If they wanted me dead, I'd already be dead."

Jordan shivered. "Do you have a plan?"

Damiano didn't reply. He lifted his eyes to the hatch. "Someone's coming."

He was right.

The hatch opened and a ladder was thrown down. A male voice barked something in Italian.

"What's he saying?" Jordan said.

"They want me to come up." Damiano got to his feet.

"Wait," Jordan said, grabbing his wrist as his heart started to pound. "You're going?"

Damiano looked at his hand oddly, the yellow light throwing shadows across his face. "Of course. I can hardly refuse. They'll just drag me out if I don't obey them." His lips twisted. "If they don't kill me, I should be back within a few hours. Let go, *bello*."

Jordan swallowed, his fingers refusing to cooperate. *Don't go*, he wanted to blurt out like a child being afraid of staying alone in the dark.

Something shifted in Damiano's expression as he studied Jordan's face.

"Close your eyes and visualize a place that makes you feel calm. Don't open your eyes until I'm back." Then he carefully extracted his hand from Jordan's grip before shrugging out of his tux jacket and throwing it to Jordan. "No point getting blood on it," he said when Jordan gave him a blank look, before turning away and climbing the ladder.

The hatch closed after him with a thud, and there was the sound of a bolt sliding into place. Locking him up.

Clutching the jacket in his hands, Jordan squeezed his eyes shut.

He breathed, in and out.

He wasn't in a tiny cellar deep underground.

He was somewhere outside, somewhere nice and a little chilly.

He wasn't in a tiny, tomb-like cellar.

He was, and no one but his captors knew where he was.

His chest tight and his heart beating so fast he felt dizzy, Jordan clutched the jacket tighter against him, burying his nose in it. It smelled nice.

It smelled of another person. A man with piercing eyes and sure hands. That man was a cold-blooded killer, but at this moment, Jordan didn't give a damn. He wanted him back. He didn't want to be left alone there, buried alive, forgotten.

*Come back.*

# Chapter 9

Jordan had no idea how much time had passed when he finally heard the hatch open. It could have been just a few hours, but it felt like a small eternity. He'd done his best to lose himself in his thoughts, but he was only partially successful, and by the time the hatch opened, he felt like he couldn't breathe, each breath a struggle, his lungs refusing to cooperate.

He stared greedily at the hatch as the ladder was thrown inside. Damiano was climbing down, moving with none of his usual grace.

One of the goons peered down and said something in Italian. He yanked the ladder up before Damiano even finished climbing down, forcing Damiano to jump off it. He did, a punched-out noise leaving his lips as he fell to the ground.

"Are you all right?" Jordan said, stumbling forward. His knees still felt too weak and shaky from his latest panic attack, but at least he was physically fine. From the way Damiano gingerly hauled himself into a sitting position, he wasn't.

"Fine," he said in a tone that suggested that the subject was closed.

Jordan narrowed his eyes, studying him carefully. Damiano's lip was split and there was an ugly bruise on his jaw, but there had to be more injuries than that. "Let me see," he said and, ignoring the stink eye he was getting, he quickly unbuttoned Damiano's shirt and pushed it off his wide shoulders.

He sucked a breath in when he saw the dark bruises all over his torso. He had been kicked in the ribs, repeatedly. "Is something broken?" he said, gingerly touching Damiano's ribs.

"Just a crack or two," Damiano said in a clipped voice. "But my shoulder is dislocated. Can you relocate it?"

Jordan winced but nodded. He spread Damiano's jacket on the floor and gestured to it. "Lie down on your back."

Damiano did, laying his injured arm away from his body at a ninety degree angle.

Crouching down beside him, Jordan grabbed his hand and slowly but firmly pulled until he finally felt the click of the bone setting into place and saw some of the tension leave Damiano's face.

"Thanks," Damiano said, closing his eyes.

Jordan stared at him for a moment. Looking down, he realized that he was still holding Damiano's hand.

Right.

He let go—and immediately became aware of the walls around him.

Fuck.

This was so pathetic. He was stronger than this.

"Who are they?" Jordan said, eyeing Damiano's hand to distract himself. It was big and fine-boned, with long, graceful fingers. The hand of a killer. "What did they want?"

Damiano didn't open his eyes. "They want me to write a will and leave everything I own to some random person. A puppet, obviously. I declined. They got a little upset."

Frowning, Jordan swept his gaze over him. He seemed more fatigued than a few cracked ribs and a dislocated shoulder should make such a physically fit man. "Are you hurt somewhere else?"

Damiano shook his head. "They mostly used waterboarding."

Right. His hair was wet. Jordan had thought it was sweat.

"Sorry," he said, grimacing. He and some of his friends had tried waterboarding for shits and giggles when they had been teenagers, and he'd never forget the sensation of drowning as water was poured over the cloth covering his mouth. He had ended up feeling claustrophobic and violently retching after just a few seconds. Damiano had been gone for so long. Jordan couldn't imagine what kind of mental strength a man must have to endure that kind of torture for more than a few minutes.

"It's unpleasant and exhausting, but nothing some rest won't fix."

"You don't have to pretend to be fine, you know," Jordan said, smiling wryly. "Your tough guy membership won't be revoked if you admit you aren't fine after hours of torture." He chuckled. "Look at me, a mess after a few hours alone in a cellar."

Damiano opened his eyes. "It had been just an hour, actually."

Jordan didn't want to believe it. It had felt like an eternity to him. "How do you know that?"

"I counted time."

Oh.

"Did it help?"

"Not really." Damiano studied him for a moment. "You're trembling."

"Of course I am," Jordan said with a laugh. "I killed four men today, I was kidnapped by some gangsters who torture people like it's nothing, and I'm locked in a tiny box underground. I'm cold, claustrophobic, and freaked out, and I really want to hold your hand, even though I really fucking dislike you. Of course I'm trembling."

Damiano stared at him as if Jordan were a strange, alien creature he'd never seen. Maybe he wasn't used to people speaking frankly and admitting weakness.

"You may hold my hand," he said at last.

"Huh. I was told you were a sociopath incapable of empathy."

Damiano actually *smiled*. "It's not inaccurate. Panic attacks are just annoying, and I don't want you to stink up the place if you throw up. If holding my hand prevents you from that, it's no big sacrifice."

"And here I was starting to think you might have a heart," Jordan said, making a show of taking Damiano's hand with great reluctance.

"I do," Damiano said, closing his eyes again. "It serves to send blood to my organs."

"No one told me you were funny." Jordan's unsteady breathing evened out a little as he squeezed Damiano's hand and found the pulse at his wrist.

At least he wasn't alone. And the fucked-up part was, he was a little glad Damiano was the person locked up with him. This man projected confidence and strength even after he was beaten up and tortured.

It made him irrationally believe everything was going to be fine.

***

Everything wasn't going fine.

Damiano was taken for torture sessions three more times that day, and each time he returned the worse for wear, even though he tried not to show it, his eyes emanating cold fury and determination despite the physical state of his body.

Jordan couldn't even lie to himself anymore: he admired that asshole. He still thought Damiano was an arrogant dick, but his strength of character was undeniable. Jordan had always admired mental strength, and he had no doubt anymore that if there was a competition for mental fortitude, Damiano would win it easily.

Jordan wasn't going to win that competition anytime soon; that was for sure. Every time Damiano was taken away, he came undone embarrassingly fast, feeling caged and panicky, scared shitless that this would be the time they would finally give up and kill Damiano, and then Jordan would be alone, only him and the four walls and darkness.

Every time Damiano was thrown back into the cellar, Jordan felt almost dizzy with sheer relief. He fixed Damiano as well as he could given their lack of resources and the stubborn man's refusal to talk about the injuries he'd sustained, and then he grabbed Damiano's hand—and breathed.

When Damiano told him that it was night by his calculations, Jordan allowed himself to hope for some respite. Surely even bad guys had to sleep at night.

When several hours passed and no one came for Damiano, Jordan finally relaxed and tried to fall asleep.

But it was impossible.

It was miserably cold, the humidity making him shiver uncontrollably on the thin bedding that those assholes dropped into the cellar the last time they had brought Damiano. The bedding was better than nothing, but it wasn't a high bar to clear.

Jordan wrapped his jacket around him as best as he could, but it wasn't much help, considering how damp it was from the humidity.

Fuck it.

He sat up and shoved his bedding close to Damiano's and snuggled up against him, ignoring the way the other man's body went rigid.

"Are you under the impression that I'm a cuddler?" Damiano said. He sounded a mix of coldly amused and irritated.

"No," Jordan said, squirming closer and throwing an arm around him. "But I don't care. I have no intention of getting pneumonia and dying before we're rescued. So suck it up. This is the smart thing to do. You know I'm right. Getting a cold would only make you weaker on top of those nasty bruises you're sporting."

"You're extremely aggravating."

"I'll take that as a compliment, coming from you." Jordan covered them both with his jacket, sighing in delight as he finally felt moderately warm for the first time since they were kidnapped. "Sleep. I won't tell anyone that we cuddled under duress." He tucked his face against Damiano's bicep and closed his eyes. Warmth. Blessed, sweet warmth. It felt impossibly good after a day of shivering in misery.

This was the safest, warmest, and calmest he'd felt since the whole ordeal started. Jordan tried not to dwell on it too much. He generally wasn't one to freak out over things. It was what it was.

Damiano remained very tense against him for a long time.

After what seemed like forever, his body slowly relaxed, his breathing evening out.

Feeling like he'd won some important battle, Jordan allowed himself to drift off.

# Chapter 10

It was amazing how much more at ease one felt with a person when one spent hours cuddled up to them.

Jordan snuggled even closer, pressing his face against Damiano's throat and breathing in deeply. One upside of waterboarding was how clean Damiano smelled despite the torture he endured every few hours. All Jordan could smell was skin and man. He wouldn't be able to identify what exactly Damiano smelled like even if his life depended on it, but he smelled good. His heartbeat was firm and steady under Jordan's hand, reminding him with its every beat that he wasn't alone.

"Get off me," Damiano said. "My bladder is killing me."

Jordan reluctantly rolled back, allowing the other man to get to his feet. He closed his eyes as Damiano took a leak.

When Damiano returned to the bedding and lay down, Jordan reached for him greedily again, laying a hand over his firm pec. His heart beat steadily under his palm.

"Do you really have claustrophobia or is it just an excuse to grope me?"

"Arrogant dick," Jordan mumbled into his bicep. Damiano's shirt was in a sorry state, and his arms were practically bare now. The firmness of his muscles calmed him, his lizard brain taking comfort in it.

There was something oddly reassuring about this man. He kind of wanted to slip his hand under Damiano's shirt and feel his heartbeat without the fabric in the way. He wondered if it would be weird.

"You can't be still cold," Damiano said tersely, but he wasn't pushing him away. He could have, if he really wanted to.

"I'm not," Jordan said. "And I don't want to become cold again. You're not afraid of a little touch, are you?"

"I'm not afraid."

Jordan almost smiled. "Then why are you so worked up?"

"I'm not worked up. I just don't do this. I don't like people touching me."

Jordan frowned. Was this really making him uncomfortable? He had thought it was just an aversion to anything remotely sentimental, but could it be something more than that?

"Do you have bad memories or something?" Jordan said. He would feel like a giant dick if that was the case.

"No. I just don't like it."

Rolling his eyes, Jordan said, "You let people touch you when you have sex." Though, come to think of it, Jordan now remembered how little Damiano had touched the redhead when she had sucked his cock. It had almost seemed as though he'd been just putting up with it.

"That's different," Damiano said.

"How is that different? Sex makes you feel good. Cuddling makes you feel good, too. Both activities are recreational and involve physical touch."

"I don't have sex to feel good." Damiano's voice was full of derision. "Sex is tension relief. It's a physiological need."

"And hugs and cuddles aren't?" Jordan said, stroking the side of Damiano's torso. "It's been scientifically proven that babies need physical touch and affection for normal development."

"I'm a grown man."

*Yes, but you were a child once.*

Jordan paused as a strange, horrible thought occurred to him. Had this man been hugged at all? Surely he couldn't be the first person to touch him like this?

He didn't ask. He didn't want to know the answer either way.

"Does this really feel unpleasant for you?" he asked instead. "Like, skin crawling, nausea, anxiety, stuff like that? Because we sure as hell can stop if it's—"

"No."

"Seriously, if it's really bothering you, I'm not that cold—"

"I already said no," Damiano said irritably. "Of course it's not physically unpleasant. I'm perfectly aware of how brain chemistry works, and the effect of oxytocin on the body."

Jordan blinked, once again reminded of the fact that this man was more than just brute strength and violence; he was also very intelligent and well educated.

"Okay," he said softly. "Then I'm not moving."

Jordan had no idea how long they lay like that before the hatch above opened again and a male voice barked something in Italian and threw down the ladder.

Jordan's arm tightened around Damiano.

He felt Damiano sigh. "Let me up. No point in annoying them or they won't give us food again."

Hating how desperate and kind of clingy he felt, Jordan let go.

He watched grimly as Damiano climbed the ladder. He did seem a little better after a night's rest, but Jordan had a bad feeling that it wouldn't last.

He counted to five thousand and forty-seven before the hatch was opened again and Damiano was carried inside by two men.

His heart in his throat, Jordan staggered to his feet. "What's wrong with him? What did you do to him?"

The assholes said something to each other before dumping wet wipes and a bucket of water on the floor. "Don't let him die," one of them said before they left.

"Damiano?"

The other man didn't reply.

His heart pounding, Jordan carefully touched Damiano, trying to see where he was wounded. He must have been seriously wounded to lose consciousness like this.

His chest looked fine. Jordan couldn't see any new bruises on top of the others he'd already had. But when he turned Damiano onto his stomach, he sucked a breath in. Damiano's back was a mess of blood and flesh, his torn shirt completely soaked with blood. They'd whipped him.

Bile rising to his throat, Jordan carefully tore off the pieces of the shirt still clinging to Damiano's back and reached for the wet wipes and the bucket.

His fingers shaking, he cleaned Damiano's back as best as he could. He applied pressure to the deepest wounds until they stopped bleeding, little by little.

But there was nothing more he could do. He didn't have an antiseptic or anything to bandage the wounds. He could only hope they didn't get infected, but he didn't have high hopes for that, considering that their environment was far from sterile.

Unfortunately, he turned out to be right.

Within an hour, Damiano was running a fever. He was delirious, muttering something under his breath in Italian.

Jordan didn't know what to do, and he utterly loathed the feeling. He was a competent man used to things always going his way. He was used to bossing people around at work, being in charge of any situation. But he felt completely out of his depth right now, like another person entirely, not the cool-headed, composed man he normally was.

"Don't die, don't die, don't die," he found himself whispering, running his fingers through Damiano's sweaty hair in his lap. He whispered it like a mantra, trying to get his breathing under control again, all the while fighting the panic clawing at his chest.

At some point—maybe hours later—the assholes returned.

Jordan glared at them. "He's in no state to be tortured," he bit out, cradling Damiano's head protectively. "He's unconscious, he has a fever! Bring me something to treat him—he needs antibiotics, bandages, painkillers!"

The men exchanged a look.

Desperation clogged Jordan's throat. "You don't want him to die, do you? You need him alive! He's burning up. He probably has an infection."

He must have convinced them, because one of them returned with some penicillin, antiseptic, and another bucket of water, as well as food.

Jordan didn't touch the food. He had no appetite and Damiano was in no state to eat. Jordan gave him some water, careful not to make him choke and rubbing his throat to make him swallow.

By the evening, or what he guessed was evening, he was exhausted. Despite the antibiotics and the constant sponge baths Jordan was giving him, Damiano's condition wasn't getting better, his fever alarmingly high, and Jordan felt more panicky by the minute.

What if he didn't have an infection but something else?

What if those assholes had kicked him too hard and he had internal bleeding?

"Don't you dare die on me," he whispered furiously, wiping sweat from Damiano's dark brow. "Imagine how pleased your family will be if you die. You're more spiteful than that, aren't you?"

Damiano didn't reply. He wasn't completely unconscious: he lifted his eyelids sometimes, looking at him with glazed, feverish eyes. Jordan wasn't sure he even recognized him, much less understood him, but Jordan still talked to him. It made him feel a little calmer. Even a delirious Damiano managed to keep the walls around them at bay.

When Jordan felt that his eyes could no longer stay open, he lay on his back and pulled Damiano half on top of him, keeping his hands on his biceps, to make sure Damiano didn't turn on his back and aggravate his wounds further.

Jesus, he was heavy.

He didn't look all that heavy—all muscle and very little fat—but he was much heavier than Jordan had expected.

He had been half afraid that he would feel crushed and claustrophobic in this position, but to his relief, he didn't. It was actually the opposite: he felt like there was a warm blanket over him, keeping the chill and the tiny room away, his world narrowing to the weight and heat of Damiano's body, hot puffs of breath against his neck, and the heartbeat against his chest. He felt completely surrounded. And warm. So very warm and grounded.

He slept like the dead.

# Chapter 11

The world was burning.

Or maybe it was him burning up. His back certainly felt on fire.

"Shh, don't thrash so much, you'll only open your wounds again."

A voice. There was someone there. A soothing male voice speaking English. Hands stroking his hair.

He wanted to tell him to stop, but his mouth didn't seem to be listening to his commands, and truth be told, the touch wasn't entirely unpleasant, distracting him from the burning pain in his back.

"Huh, you like it. Who knew you could be tamed with something as simple as hair-petting?"

Damiano shook his head, trying to claw his way to consciousness, but the pain was just too intense to allow him to focus, and instead, he slipped into darkness.

The next time he became semi-awake, his hair was being stroked again.

"I can't believe I'm doing this," the same male voice said. "Petting your hair and cuddling your head against my chest. If only people in my department could see me now." He laughed a little, but there was a broken, tight edge to it. "Don't die. Please. I don't think I can do it alone. I'm losing my mind already."

Darkness again.

Fire. Fire eating his flesh from the inside. Fire burning along his back. The taste of ash in his mouth.

"What's wrong? What is it? Are you thirsty? Is that it?"

Cool water against his burning, parched lips.

"Easy there," the man said, stroking his hair. "That's enough, we don't want you to throw up again, though I don't think you have anything to throw up in your stomach. Now sleep. You need to sleep—and wake up. Please." The voice broke on the last word.

Darkness. Pain. Fire. Gentle hands stroking his hair and the same voice whispering nonsense, sometimes angry and tired, sometimes pleading and shaky.

"It's all your fucking fault, you know. If you didn't get me so worked up, I wouldn't have overslept. I would have gone to the wedding, and you would be here, alone, dying without anyone to look after you—and—and..."

Darkness. Pain. Fire licking his insides. Fingers stroking his hair.

"I think I'm losing my mind. I'm not sure I'm even sleeping anymore or how much time has passed. I can't—I can't do this. I can't breathe in here. I need you to wake up." A shaky kiss pressed to the top of his head. Ragged breaths that sounded almost like sobs. "I need you to wake up. I need—I need you."

***

Jordan had no idea how much he'd slept this time, but he jerked awake, panicky. He knew that something was different even before he fully woke up.

It took him a moment to realize what was different.

Damiano's body on top of him was no longer burning up.

"*Buongiorno*," Damiano said into his neck, his voice rough like sandpaper. "Is there a reason I'm lying on top of you? Do I have to be worried for my virtue?"

Jordan grinned, feeling so relieved he didn't know what to do with himself. He blinked, trying to get rid of the sudden wetness in his eyes. He was just tired; that was all.

"Don't flatter yourself," he said, adopting a dry, snarky tone that hopefully didn't betray how raw he was still feeling. "What you need to be worried about is getting pissed on, because my bladder really didn't appreciate having two hundred pounds of dead weight on it for hours."

"It's two hundred and ten, actually," Damiano said, and didn't move.

Jordan would be perfectly content to keep lying like this too, except he wasn't kidding about his bladder. He had been so stressed that his body's needs had entirely slipped his mind.

"I'm serious," Jordan said. "Get off me, you."

Damiano sighed and rolled off him.

"Careful!" Jordan said, supporting him. "I didn't play nurse for you for days only to have you ruin my hard work."

Damiano gave him a long look, but he did move more carefully as he stretched on his stomach on the thin, lumpy bedding. "This is a lot less comfortable," he grumbled.

"No kidding," Jordan said, walking to the toilet and unzipping his pants. "You're welcome, by the way."

There was a long silence that was only broken by the sound of Jordan relieving his bladder.

Fuck, it felt good.

He was zipping his pants when he heard a quiet, "Thanks."

Jordan blinked at the wall. He had a feeling it wasn't a word Damiano used often.

Feeling a little off-balance, Jordan did his best to rinse his mouth with water to get rid of the stale morning breath.

"You need water," he said, pouring some into a cup and grabbing the antibiotics. "And you probably need the antibiotics again, though I have no idea how much time has passed since the last time I was able to give you some."

Damiano hauled himself into a sitting position, his muscles bulging as he did so. Jordan eyed his physique, musing on the unfairness of the genetic lottery. If only everyone could look this good after being tortured and being sick and feverish for days.

"Water," Damiano said eagerly, and Jordan was suddenly struck by how open and unguarded his face was compared to the arrogant man with an inscrutable expression that he had met. Had it really been just four or five days ago? It felt like it had been in another life.

Jordan helped him drink, brushing the dark hair off Damiano's sweaty forehead with the other hand.

He froze a little, realizing what he'd just done. He'd become so used to touching Damiano's hair—touching his everything—while he had been feverish that it came as second nature now.

Jordan cleared his throat a little.

"You need a haircut," he said, trying to act as though there was nothing unusual about his behavior. "Though you're totally rocking the Ben Barnes look, it's not very practical when you get locked up in a dungeon and tortured for days."

Damiano was looking at him with a strange expression Jordan couldn't quite read.

Rubbing the back of his neck with his hand, Jordan glanced at the toilet. "Do you need to piss? I can help you."

Damiano gave him a pinched look. "I'm not an invalid." He gingerly got to his feet, swayed, and glared at Jordan when he attempted to catch him. "I'm fine. I can take a few steps on my own."

Rolling his eyes, Jordan flopped back on the bedding. "Suit yourself," he said, closing his eyes. He still felt tired and sleepy.

He must have dozed off, because he was only distantly aware of the sound of a toilet being flushed, and then Damiano lay down—on top of him.

Jordan grunted but didn't protest. He knew how uncomfortable it was to lie on one's stomach on that thin bedding. This felt so much nicer. This was what he'd gotten used to over the past few days.

"I'm glad you aren't dead," Jordan mumbled sleepily, his brain-to-mouth filter gone. "Thanks for not dying."

He felt Damiano go still on top of him.

He didn't say anything, and Jordan drifted off.

# Chapter 12

The following days were some of the most bizarre in Jordan's life.

The assholes upstairs mostly left them alone after Jordan told them Damiano was still near his deathbed — they only dropped them food and water several times a day.

Jordan was perfectly content with that. In fact, he was pretty content in general, which was… bizarre. His panic attacks were gone. The walls had mostly stopped closing in on him, if he didn't focus on them. Maybe he'd just gotten used to the cellar.

Or more likely, it had something to do with the fact that he spent practically every waking moment wrapped up in Damiano—sometimes very literally.

Damiano's back was better now, but he still slept half on top of him, his heavy arm thrown over Jordan's chest in a manner that seemed… Jordan couldn't find a word for it. Either way, Jordan couldn't bring himself to mind. When his world was a dark, tiny room deep underground, it was Damiano's presence—his body, his hands, his voice—that kept him sane. The only thing to focus on.

Jordan was acutely aware that he was rapidly developing some kind of… unhealthy attachment, a dependency that he should have nipped in the bud, but there was nothing he could do about it.

There was nothing else in this cellar but them. No phones, no Internet, no entertainment. Just them, entangled in each other 24/7. His days started and ended with Damiano. He was the first thing on his mind when he woke up and the last thing when he fell asleep. Lack of privacy and constant physical contact erased any boundaries between them, to an alarming degree.

Everything about this man was now comforting: his low voice, his wry humor, even his scent, which was fucked-up, because after days in this cellar, neither of them objectively smelled great. Apparently, the scent of a man's sweat could seem nice and comforting in the right—or wrong—circumstances. To his embarrassment, Jordan found himself seeking out the scent of Damiano's sweat. When Damiano was asleep, Jordan buried his face into Damiano's underarm, feeling drunk on the spicy raw smell of him, the undiluted scent on his tongue.

Jordan didn't know what Damiano thought about his clinginess—if he even shared it. Damiano wasn't claustrophobic like him. He didn't need Jordan to be his anchor. But he seemed content enough to be all over Jordan's personal space, treating him like his personal pillow and allowing Jordan to play with his hair.

Jordan had no idea if Damiano remembered all the nonsense he'd told him while he had a fever—he hoped not—but it was undeniable that Damiano was significantly… mellower and handsier with him than he had been before the whipping. His reservations about cuddling certainly seemed nowhere to be seen, and he said nothing about Jordan's new propensity for stroking his hair.

Whatever.

Jordan decided to just roll with it.

During those long hours in the semi-darkness, they talked. Damiano told him a little about his childhood, mostly amusing anecdotes that weren't too personal but hinted at the lonely childhood he'd had, because there were never any friends in them.

Jordan avoided talking about his childhood. Damiano still thought he was Nate, Raffaele's boyfriend, and Jordan didn't really feel like making up stories about Nate's childhood. His own childhood stories wouldn't really fit, because he grew up in a different environment from Nate.

He kind of wanted to tell Damiano his real name, but he was a man of his word—he had promised Raffaele to play the role, so he would. It wasn't just about him, after all; it was a matter of Nate's safety.

Not that he didn't trust Damiano. The problem was, he currently trusted him *too* much, his hindbrain incapable of grasping that this man was anything but nice, wonderful, and safe.

He had to remind himself on an hourly basis that Damiano wasn't actually this nice. In the real world that existed outside this tiny room, he was a cold-hearted, ruthless son-of-a-bitch.

So they mostly ended up talking about nonsense.

"You really don't have a nickname?" Jordan said, threading his fingers through the hair on Damiano's nape.

"Really."

"Everyone has a nickname."

"I don't."

"I can give you one," Jordan said, smiling. "What about Dami?"

"If you want me to kill you, sure."

"Hmm… Anno, Danno?"

"No."

"Dino?"

Damiano snorted into his neck. "Like dinosaur?"

"All right, that wasn't one of my brighter ideas. What about Dom?"

"How is Dom a nickname for Damiano? You English are so weird with your nicknames."

"I'm American."

"There's a difference?"

"There was a war over it and everything. Look it up sometime."

Damiano hummed.

After a moment's silence, he said, "What do you call Raffaele?"

Jordan's mind went blank. The urge to tell him the truth was so strong this time that he had to literally bite his tongue.

"Rafe," he said after a moment, his stomach clenching with guilt. The fact that he felt guilt at all was ridiculous and spoke of how disturbingly strong this attachment had become. He'd met the guy a week ago, for fuck's sake. He shouldn't feel like he was betraying his bosom friend by not telling him the truth.

"Sounds stupid," Damiano said, his teeth worrying Jordan's neck.

Jordan squirmed, shivering. "What are you doing?"

"I'm hungry."

"Please don't tell me you're a cannibal on top of being a sociopath."

"All right. I won't." Damiano bit him on the neck.

Jordan laughed, because obviously it was a joke. Right?

"Stop that," Jordan said. There! He was setting some boundaries!

Damiano only bit harder, making hot pain shoot through Jordan's neck.

"I feel like your chew toy," he complained, raking his fingers through Damiano's hair, but he didn't push him away. "But yeah, I'm hungry, too."

He'd never felt hunger like this in his life.

The first few days the meager food they were given didn't bother him all that much, but with each passing day, the gnawing pit in his stomach only increased. His stomach was cramping with hunger pains and his mouth now watered at the thought of food. He was a pretty tall, physically fit guy. His body normally needed a lot of food. Damiano was bigger than him. Coupled with the fact that he was still recovering from brutal physical torture and a subsequent fever, his body probably needed more fuel than normal.

"Don't eat me," Jordan said, though he kind of wouldn't mind having something to chew on, too. Something—anything—to fill up his mouth and make him forget about putting food into it. He wondered if it would be too weird to suck on Damiano's fingers.

Damiano gave a soft snort into his neck. "I usually hear the opposite."

Jordan laughed. "I bet you do. But seriously, I hope the biting doesn't mean you're discovering your dormant cannibalistic tendencies."

"All humans are capable of cannibalism in extreme circumstances," Damiano said, moving his mouth lower and biting the juncture between his neck and shoulder. "Luckily for you, I'm not that desperate yet."

"What happens when you get that desperate?"

"You'll have to wait and find out," Damiano said.

Jordan smiled.

Nonsensical conversations like that had one big downside: they eroded the boundaries between them even more and made Jordan feel like he could tell Damiano even the most nonsensical things—and humanized Damiano. It made him feel like Damiano wouldn't lie to him. He could no longer see him as the psychopath people said he was. It seemed like nonsense.

"Do you really not love anyone?" Jordan asked on the sixth or seventh day of their captivity—it was hard to tell for sure how much time had passed when one day bled into the next and Damiano was the only thing in his world.

"I don't," Damiano said, his breath brushing against Jordan's cheek. His answer sounded half-assed, as if it wasn't the topic he was interested in and he wanted to move on to something else.

"That seems… lonely."

Damiano didn't say anything.

"Don't you believe in love?" Jordan said. He wasn't sure why he was pushing. He told himself he was just bored and conversation was the only way to pass the time, but the truth was, he *burned* to know more about this man, understand what had shaped him and made him tick.

Damiano was silent for so long Jordan thought he was ignoring him or had fallen asleep.

That was why he was so startled when Damiano actually answered him.

"I do believe in love," he said, his tone flat. "That it exists. And happens to other people."

Jordan winced. He had no idea what to say.

"Did you ever meet Raffaele's father?" Damiano said.

"No," Jordan replied honestly. He knew Nate hadn't met him, either. "Raffaele told me he wasn't a faithful husband. Is that why you are so cynical about love?"

Damiano chuckled. "No. Marco wasn't faithful to Raffaele's mother because he didn't give a damn about her. He was madly in love with my mother. He loved her so much that he kept me around, the filthy *bastardo* and product of her rape, because I was still her son, even if she hated me enough to kill herself. I was what was left of her, so he tolerated having me around, despite me being the living reminder of what happened to her."

Oh.

Jordan's gut clenched in sympathy. How would it feel to grow up in such an unloving environment, knowing that he was the reason for his mother's suicide and being hated by the man raising you?

He stroked Damiano's hair gently. "Is that why you keep people at a distance? You don't want what happened to your mother and Marco to happen to you and your loved ones?"

Damiano didn't answer.

But Jordan didn't need him to. He knew this man well enough by now to know that his silence was pretty much a confirmation. And it broke his heart a little.

"Do you still have no idea who kidnapped us?" Jordan asked, changing the subject. He didn't like how compassionate he was feeling toward this man. Jordan wasn't sure how objective his observations were when his rational thinking was so compromised. It was possible that he was just projecting.

"I have some idea," Damiano said into his ear.

Shivering, Jordan turned his head and pressed their cheeks together, not even minding the way Damiano's scruff prickled his face. He'd never had much facial hair himself, shaving just once a week.

"Yeah? Who?"

Damiano took a moment to reply. "We should find out soon enough," he said. "They gave up on torturing me for a reason."

Jordan frowned. "You were—are—still too injured to keep torturing."

A soft snort.

"I doubt they care about it. If they stopped, that means they're changing their tactics soon. Maybe they *are* waiting for me to recover enough to try new and more inventive methods of torture—or they were simply told to wait until their boss arrives, who will make the decision once he's here. The second option is more likely. Whether they'll torture me some more or kill me, their boss would want to be here personally for that. He wouldn't want to miss the opportunity to at least gloat before he gives up on getting my money and kills me."

Jordan pressed his lips together, his stomach churning heavily. He wasn't sure what disturbed him more: what Damiano was saying or the dry, careless tone of voice he used. "Aren't you scared at all?" he said, threading his fingers through Damiano's hair.

"What—of dying?"

"Yes."

Damiano made a contemplative noise. "I don't want to die because I don't like losing, but everyone dies eventually. Only people who are emotionally attached to someone are scared of death—because they are leaving behind people who need them. I don't have such a weakness."

Jordan felt a pang of infinite sadness for this man and tried to quash the ridiculous urge to hug him close.

"My baby brother went missing last year," he said, looking at the crack in the ceiling.

He knew he probably shouldn't be telling Damiano this—it would be easy to find out that Nate didn't have a baby brother if Damiano bothered to run the most basic background check. But he needed to say it. To tell him something real. "By now everyone presumes he's dead." Jordan swallowed. "And frankly, he probably is. But just because he died and left all of us heartbroken doesn't make love a weakness. Aiden might be gone, but we had twenty years with him. Memories. Even if he's dead, he lives on in our memories. Mom still celebrated his birthday this year— it's not less of a cause for celebration just because he's gone."

"So what's the moral of the story?" Damiano's voice was extremely dry. "That love isn't a weakness?"

"No," Jordan said, closing his eyes. "It absolutely can be a weakness. Personally, I'm not a fan of showing much emotion at work myself—it can be perceived as weakness by my... co-workers." *Subordinates*, Jordan nearly said, but the issue had been relevant back when he'd been a simple programmer too. When he'd started working for the Caldwell Group, he'd had to pretend to be an aloof, emotionless asshole because he didn't want to be a young, hot piece of ass for his co-workers to thirst over. He'd played that role for so long that sometimes it felt more authentic than his normal self.

Jordan sighed. "But love can be a strength, too. Something to live for when you feel down. Life can beat you up, but it's people who love you that give you the strength to pick yourself up." He had felt like shit after his divorce, but going to his mother and letting himself be babied for a few days had made him feel so much better. There was nothing quite like his mom's hugs, no matter how old he was.

His heart clenched as he remembered that Damiano had never known what it felt like to have a mother's loving embrace around him. All he had were stories—of his mother rejecting him and hating him. Jesus. No wonder he had turned out the way he was.

"And it's not true that no one needs you," Jordan said, threading his fingers through Damiano's hair. "I do."

Damiano tensed up on top of him. "All you need is a crutch to deal with your claustrophobia," he said, his voice hard and nasty. "Don't worry, the moment I'm dead, you'll be taken out of here and returned to Raffaele for ransom. They aren't risking contacting anyone while I'm alive. So you should hope that they'll kill me. When I'm dead, you can live your happily ever after."

"God, you're such an asshole," Jordan said, yanking at Damiano's hair. "I don't want you dead, you ass. I don't want to be saved if that means you're dead." Frankly, the mere thought made his stomach knot up. It was fucking scary how badly he needed Damiano to be okay. How attached to him he'd gotten.

Damiano was very still against him. "Then you're an idiot," he said at last.

Jordan smiled humorlessly. "I know."

He was perfectly aware what a terrible idea this attachment was.

But he had no idea how to remove it. Its roots were already too deep to be pulled out.

# Chapter 13

Damiano Conte had never been so unsettled in his life, and the fact that he had been betrayed, kidnapped, and tortured had little to do with it.

It was the American.

He befuddled him.

*It's not true that no one needs you. I do.*

Try as he might, he couldn't find an ulterior motive in his actions or words. The guy didn't have to treat his injuries or take care of him while he had been feverish and delirious. Damiano had never been one to rely on another person, no matter how dire the situation was. He simply didn't trust anyone enough to do it.

But somehow, over the past nine days in the basement, Raffaele's boyfriend had managed to slip past his guard.

Damiano wouldn't go as far as to say that he *trusted* him. He trusted no one. But he didn't distrust him, either. It was hard to distrust the man who had treated his injuries with such gentleness and allowed him to use him as a glorified mattress in order not to aggravate his back—while he stroked Damiano's hair. The latter felt... nice.

Nice. What an inadequate word for the strange feeling that curled in his chest every time the other man played with his hair. Damiano didn't like the sensation. The warmth it caused. It was overwhelming. Disconcerting.

It was disconcerting how quickly he'd grown used to it over the course of his illness, how much better it made him feel, distracting him from the agonizing pain.

But it was one thing to put up with such touch when his mind had been muddled with pain and fever; it was another to keep tolerating it once he recovered. To keep *anticipating* the touch. To start *wanting* it. It irritated Damiano to no end, the craving he'd developed for something so pathetic, but it wasn't as though he could put some distance between them when they were in a tiny basement little bigger than a bathroom.

*That's bullshit, and you know it*, a voice said at the back of his mind. *If you really wanted to get rid of him, you could have killed him. Choked him in his sleep. Slit his throat with a fork. Stuck the fork in his femoral artery and watched him bleed out. Or dozens of other options. Instead, you're cuddling him and letting him pet you like a cat.*

Damiano scowled, rubbing his face against the other man's throat.

He felt his pulse against his mouth. He wanted to *bite*, sink his teeth there until he reached blood, until he could taste him and find out what he was made of.

There was a peculiarity to his thoughts and desires, a base quality that would be unsettling had Damiano already not been unsettled by the situation.

"What are you thinking about?" Nate said, carding his fingers through his hair.

"I was thinking about how easy it would be to kill you."

The impossible man *chuckled*, as if Damiano had said something funny.

He had no idea.

He had no idea who he was cuddling with.

"It's a good thing I know that you aren't going to kill me."

How did he know that? Damiano knew no such thing. The more he grew accustomed to all this touchy-feely shit, the more twitchy he got. This was a potential weakness someone could exploit. If their kidnappers got any inkling about this, they might try to use it. Every moment he spent all over this man increased the likelihood of someone seeing them like this—and getting the wrong impression that he cared about him. The smart thing to do would have been to nip this shit in the bud, but after more than a week of this, he was loath to give it up.

That in itself was alarming. Obviously he knew the science behind pleasure derived from physical touch: it was all about dopamine, oxytocin and serotonin produced by the brain and giving the person a high. It was no different from drug addiction, and he despised addicts.

Maybe he should just kill the guy. It would be so easy to wrap his hands around his throat and squeeze, watch the life go out from those blue eyes as he writhed under Damiano, gasping and begging him to stop.

"How is your back?" Strong but gentle hands raked his nape and stroked the tops of his shoulders, careful not to touch his back.

"Fine," Damiano said shortly, his eyes closing from how good the touch felt.

A long-suffering sigh. "I know you're fine. But do you feel better today than you did yesterday? Come on, give me something to work with."

"Why do you care?" Damiano said, finally asking the question that had been on his mind for the past week since his whipping—and had become only more persistent since their conversation last night.

*I don't want you dead. I don't want to be saved if that means you're dead.*

The words still kept ringing in his ears, infuriatingly distracting.

The hands stopped stroking him.

Damiano frowned in displeasure.

"I know this is weird," the other man said, clearing his throat a little. "I know it probably isn't real—just the circumstances, forced proximity, my phobia, and the stress—but... I care for you. I feel safe with you. I don't want you to die or get hurt—ow, stop that!"

Damiano bit him on the neck again, just to shut him up.

Apparently words could cause a dopamine high, too. What an unpleasant discovery.

"Ahh, you're hurting me."

*Good,* Damiano thought, giving him another vicious bruise. He deserved to be hurt for saying inane shit like that. He wished the room weren't so dark and he could see the bruises all over that pale neck.

"Damiano," was a breathless whisper as fingers buried in his hair again. Not pushing him away. Pulling him closer.

And Damiano went, sucking new bruises into his skin.

Fuck, he couldn't wait to be rid of him.

# Chapter 14

The sounds of gunshots woke Jordan up.

His heart pounding, he sat up. "Damiano?"

"I'm here," Damiano said from behind him.

He found Damiano leaned against the wall, trying to get into his tux jacket, a pained grimace on his face.

"What are you doing?" Jordan shot to his feet. "You're going to reopen your wounds!"

"Help me put it on," Damiano said, in a tone that brooked no argument.

Frowning, Jordan helped him reluctantly. Some of the wounds on Damiano's back had barely scabbed over because they kept opening every time he moved. "Why?"

"If I'm right and Lorenzo doesn't fuck up, we're about to get rescued," Damiano said.

Jordan's heart jumped to his throat. He racked his brain, trying to remember who Lorenzo was before finally remembering the stony-faced older guy who followed Damiano around and bossed his security detail. Some kind of right-hand man? Head of security? Something along those lines.

"And why do you need to put on your tux for that?" Jordan said. "Will Lorenzo faint if he sees you bare-chested?"

"Appearances are everything," Damiano said, his eyes hard and distant. "He can't see me as weak. He can't know that I'm injured—that I have been whipped."

"I thought he was your right-hand man or something?"

"He is."

Jordan looked away, feeling a jolt of sadness. What a lonely existence it must have been if Damiano didn't even trust his right hand…

"How do you know it's your people and not someone else?" Jordan said, trying to fix his own clothes. It was a lost cause.

"The timing is right. It's been ten days, enough time for the traitor to relax and come see me personally without being afraid of being followed—or so they would think. Lorenzo was supposed to have everyone in the family followed 24/7. As soon as someone behaved suspiciously, he would have tailed them until they brought him to our location."

Jordan stared at him. "It was a trap? You organized the whole thing?"

Damiano smiled grimly. "You give me too much credit. But it was a possibility. I discussed it with Lorenzo and he knew what to do if I got kidnapped."

It came to him slowly. "You wanted to lull them into a false sense of security after you were so lenient with Andrea. That's why you let him live."

"Yes," Damiano said. "I knew Andrea wasn't the only one plotting against me. There was someone else acting independently from him. Someone more subtle and cautious. I wanted to draw them out." Damiano smiled. "Sometimes inspiring too much fear can be detrimental. By letting Andrea live, I made myself look more merciful than I am. That made them less cautious."

"Great plan," Jordan said, glaring at him. "And what if they killed you? Weren't you scared at all?"

"I knew they wanted to kidnap me more than they wanted to kill me. Our attackers were trying very hard to avoid shooting me anywhere vital. They wanted to take me alive. If they wanted to kill me, I would be dead."

The sounds of gunshots sounded a lot closer now.

Jordan tensed up, watching the hatch with his heart in his throat. What if Damiano was wrong and it wasn't his people?

*What if he was right?*

When the hatch opened, it was Lorenzo's square-jawed face squinting down at them. "Damiano?" he said uncertainly.

Jordan breathed out and looked at Damiano. He was a little unsettled when he saw that all emotion was gone from Damiano's face. His face hardened, his eyes turning cold and unreadable, his posture straightening. He said something in Italian, his voice not loud but distinctly unimpressed.

Lorenzo was clearly uncomfortable. His tone was apologetic as he replied, and then he threw down the ladder.

Biting the inside of his cheek to stop himself from saying something, Jordan watched as Damiano confidently walked to the ladder and climbed it, as if his back wasn't still a mess. He must have been in a great deal of pain, but his face betrayed nothing. Lorenzo probably had no clue that his boss was holding himself up with sheer will.

Jordan climbed the ladder after Damiano, his hands shaking as it hit him:

It was over.

Everything was over.

He hauled himself up onto the floor above and looked around, momentarily disoriented by the brightness and noise. The first thing his gaze focused on was the body on the floor. A fresh corpse with a bullet in his gut. It was one of the men who normally brought them food.

Bile rising in his throat, Jordan wrenched his gaze away and looked around. They still seemed to be underground, judging by the lack of windows.

He exhaled when he finally saw Damiano speaking to Lorenzo down the corridor. Lorenzo nodded, handed Damiano a gun, and they walked away together.

Jordan stared after them unseeingly for a moment, not understanding. Were they leaving him behind? Damiano didn't even glance back at him.

His stomach in knots, Jordan followed after them slowly, not sure what else to do. He kept his eyes firmly on Damiano's nape, to avoid looking at the bodies littering the floor.

They ascended the stairs to what Jordan assumed was the first floor of the building: bright sunlight was coming through the windows.

In the middle of a luxurious living room, Gustavo was bound to a chair, with two men guarding him.

When Damiano saw his cousin, his blank expression didn't change. Jordan had no idea if he was surprised or not as he stared at Gustavo. At last, he said something in Italian, his voice quiet.

Gustavo glared at him with such venom Jordan was taken aback. Gustavo had seemed like such a quiet, unassuming guy. He was the last person on his mind when Jordan had contemplated who could be behind their kidnapping. He had thought it might be Paolo, who had expressed bitterness and envy toward Damiano, not the guy who had seemed more concerned with his phone than power games. Showed what he knew.

Sneering, Gustavo spat out something, and the only word Jordan could understand was "*bastardo*." It hardly needed a translation.

Damiano looked at Gustavo for a moment.

Then he lifted his gun and shot him between his eyes.

Turning to Lorenzo, he said something, completely ignoring the corpse of his so-called relative at his feet.

Jordan swallowed, Ferrara's words suddenly echoing in his ears. *He's a high-functioning sociopath. He's the type of person who can casually pull out a gun and shoot all of us at the table and then go back to his dinner.*

He hadn't really believed it then. But now…

Jordan stared at Damiano's profile, hating how badly a part of him still wanted his attention.

He was free.

He shouldn't need this man anymore. He didn't need him anymore.

He was Jordan Gates, a grown-ass, self-sufficient man, not the clingy, claustrophobic mess he had been for the last ten days.

He repeated that as a mantra as Damiano's people cleared the mansion and got into black cars.

For a moment, Jordan thought he had been forgotten entirely, but then one of the goons none-too-gently grabbed his arm and shoved him into one of the cars. It wasn't the car Damiano was in.

It was fine. Fine.

He didn't need him anymore.

# Chapter 15

Damiano closed his eyes as he listened to Lorenzo's report.

The road that normally seemed flawless now felt like the bumpiest ride he'd ever experienced. Every jolt of the car was like torture—and he knew a thing or two about torture. It didn't help that he was leaning back against the seat and the fabric of his tux was aggravating his wounds. But that was his normal posture and anything else would be noted by Lorenzo as unusual.

It was jarring how taxing this inability to relax was after ten days with his guard down. He'd gotten too comfortable. Dangerously comfortable.

"You're sure Gustavo was working alone?" he said.

"Almost certainly," Lorenzo answered. "I had all the family members tracked, as you ordered. No one behaved suspiciously bar Gustavo. Well, there's that thing with Raffaele, but it's not relevant."

Damiano opened his eyes. "Raffaele? What about him?"

Lorenzo snorted. "Looks like he has another boytoy on the side. I've listened in to some snatches of his phone calls and they were pretty damning. No wonder he wasn't all that freaked out over his boyfriend's disappearance."

"He wasn't?" Damiano looked out the window at the passing scenery. "That's odd. I thought you reported that it was supposedly a… love match."

"That's what my source in Boston said," Lorenzo said with a shrug. "I didn't investigate it myself. Maybe he was wrong. Or maybe Raffaele's feelings didn't last. I've always been skeptical about this supposed love when he'd always had one-night stands in the past. Do you want me to investigate it myself?"

Yes.

"No," Damiano said, quashing his inner voice ruthlessly. The less he knew, the better. He shouldn't feed this… little attachment he had developed for Raffaele's boyfriend. If he ignored it—and him—it would die, as all things did.

Lorenzo continued his report, focusing on the new deals and financial reports this time.

Damiano listened only with half an ear. His back bothered him more than he would have liked—but Lorenzo's information was somehow more aggravating.

Raffaele was a fucking idiot if he was cheating.

His own anger surprised him. He usually scoffed at the notion of cheating. A person's body belonged only to said person, and the concept of betraying someone if one chose to share their body with someone else had always seemed bizarre to him.

But he knew other people weren't built like he was. Nate would probably be upset if he found out.

*Even if he does find out, it's not your place to tell him. Stay out of it.*

*Stay away.*

*He's not yours to take care of.*

He never was.

***

When they arrived at the villa, it was evening already.

Damiano gritted his teeth as he got out of the car stiffly.

"You all right, boss?" Lorenzo said, frowning.

Damiano shot him a cold look. "Of course," he ground out. Hopefully the wounds hadn't opened again and blood hadn't seeped through his tux yet. Judging by the fact that Lorenzo was already turning away, Damiano looked better than he felt.

The sounds of the cars parking behind them made him stiffen.

He wanted to look back. Just to make sure his orders were carried out and Nate hadn't been forgotten. But of course his orders had been carried out. They always were.

Damiano didn't turn around.

He watched Raffaele emerge out of the villa. His stern face changed very little when he saw Damiano, but when he looked at something behind him, there was clear relief in his black eyes.

Damiano's lips curled into a derisive sneer. How touching. So apparently his stepbrother did care about his boyfriend's well-being even if he was cheating on him. Truly a love story for the ages.

Giving him a curt nod, Raffaele marched forward.

Damiano strode toward the house, ignoring the burning pain in his back. He had no desire to watch them kiss or something equally nauseating.

"I'd be more careful, boss," Lorenzo said, catching up to him. "You might shoot your leg."

Damiano gave him a blank look before realizing that he had his finger on the trigger of his gun. Slowly, he took the finger off and turned the safety on.

He was calm.

He was calm and collected.

He had nothing to be angry about.

# Chapter 16

Jordan had to shower with the door open.

His chest tight, he watched the water beat down on his body, washing away the grime, sweat, and Damiano's blood.

Jordan would have liked to say that he felt like his old self after the shower, but that would have been a lie. He felt clean, which was a big improvement, but the anxiety and the sense of displacement remained.

The world still didn't seem real. Everything felt slightly off: the scents, the sounds, the colors.

His spacious room made him feel distinctly uncomfortable: it felt too big and open. Unsafe.

And that was the crux of the problem, wasn't it?

He felt unsafe, despite being saved.

"Are you all right?" Ferrara said stiffly, glancing at Jordan before his eyes returned to his laptop.

"Sure," Jordan said, dropping his towel and pulling on a T-shirt and shorts. He couldn't bring himself to care that he was naked in front of his boss. Actually, some embarrassment would have been very welcome. Anything would have been better than this anxiety and sense of wrongness. He kept waiting to finally feel safe—feel *normal*—but the feeling remained elusive.

"You're lying," Ferrara stated, his gaze on his laptop. "I will pay for the services of a therapist once we return to Boston. That's the least I can do. It's my fault for not waking you up and forcing you to catch a ride with Damiano." He grimaced. "I could sense that something was going to happen, so I figured it would be better if you missed the wedding, but it only messed everything up."

"You couldn't have known," Jordan said tonelessly.

"Still." Ferrara went silent, typing on his laptop. "I bought tickets home for tomorrow. Noon."

Jordan didn't say anything. He wanted his boss gone from his room, but he knew Ferrara should be here to keep the appearance of a concerned lover reunited with his missing boyfriend.

There was a knock on the door, and Jordan whipped his head toward it.

It was a maid. She brought him food.

Lots of food. Fifteen different dishes.

"This is too much," Jordan said, eyeing the feast in front of him. He was hungry, but he knew his stomach wouldn't be able to handle more than some soup after ten days of being half-starved. "You shouldn't have."

Ferrara frowned. "It's not me. The cook probably feels bad for you."

Jordan played with the food listlessly. He forced himself to eat some soup and bread and to drink a few glasses of water.

There was another knock on the door, and Jordan held his breath again.

It was a security guy. He handed Ferrara a package.

"This is for you," Ferrara said, turning to Jordan. "A new phone to replace the one you lost."

Jordan accepted it without a comment.

It was only a matter of minutes to get the phone set up and have his data restored from the cloud. If only his mental state could have been fixed as easily.

He wanted Damiano.

Jordan screwed his eyes shut and breathed, trying to erase the thought from his mind.

It didn't work.

Rationally, he understood that this attachment, this dependency, was born in unnatural circumstances that had nothing to do with their real lives. It was a combination of his desperate need for an anchor when his claustrophobia was driving him crazy, some fucked-up nurse-patient attachment from caring for Damiano for days, and the false sense of intimacy caused by the constant physical contact. Now that they were back in the real world, he knew that what he had felt in captivity wasn't real. As a rational man, Jordan understood that.

It changed very little.

He still thought about him constantly, obsessively, wondering if he was okay, if he got professional medical help. From the rigidly straight way Damiano had held himself as he had emerged out of the car, Jordan wouldn't put it past him not to tough it out in order not to reveal his weakness in front of his underlings. Stubborn ass.

*Enough. Stop fixating on him. It's not real. You should worry about your real loved ones, not about a man you've known for less than two weeks.*

"How did you keep my family from learning that I was missing?" Jordan said, his gut clenching as he realized how bad it would have been if they found out about it. After what happened to Aiden, his parents might not have recovered from a second blow like that. "I was supposed to return home a week ago."

Ferrara's brows furrowed. "I'm aware of what happened to your brother, so I was hesitant about contacting your parents and upsetting them prematurely. I told Nate to message your mother and tell her you loved Italy so much that you decided to extend your stay. Maybe we should have told them the truth, but I was reasonably sure you would be ransomed—"

"No, I'm glad you didn't tell them. My parents would have just worried needlessly."

Silence fell.

"Do you know what he did to Gustavo?" Ferrara said.

Jordan froze. "What do you mean?" he said, without looking at him.

"Gustavo disappeared. He isn't answering calls and his people have no idea where he is. It can't be a coincidence that Damiano returned just as Gustavo disappeared."

Jordan stared at his phone's screen unseeingly. "What makes you think I would know anything?"

He could feel Ferrara's heavy gaze on him. "You're right. Forget it."

Guilt churned in his gut.

The worst part was, he felt guilty only about not telling Ferrara the truth—he had been brought to Italy to help him, after all. But he didn't feel much of anything about the cold-blooded murder he'd witnessed. Gustavo was a two-faced asshole who had betrayed and tortured Damiano for days. He was hardly an innocent bystander. Still. Shouldn't he feel more disturbed by what he'd seen? He definitely shouldn't have been worrying about the murderer.

Jordan cleared his throat a little. "It wasn't Damiano behind the attacks on you and Nate."

Ferrara bored his eyes into him. "And how do you know that?"

"He told me."

"He told you." Ferrara couldn't have sounded more skeptical and pitying if he tried.

Jordan glared at his food. "I know what you're thinking. But that's why you brought me here: to observe and help you find the traitor. So you'll have to trust my observational skills, *sir*. He wasn't lying when he told me that. It wasn't him."

Ferrara said nothing, but Jordan could feel his assessing, curious gaze on him for the rest of the evening.

Whatever. He'd kept his part of the deal. If Ferrara didn't believe him, it was his problem.

"I will sleep on the couch," Ferrara informed him, insufferably bossy, as always.

Jordan shrugged and got into the bed.

He closed his eyes as he listened to the sounds of another person preparing for sleep.

Then the lights were turned off and the room went dark.

Jordan breathed deeply, trying to turn his brain off and fall asleep. He counted sheep. He tried to empty his mind and think of nothing. He used every tactic he knew of.

It didn't work.

Ferrara's breathing soon evened out, but Jordan couldn't say the same about his own. Little by little, his panic increased. The bed was so soft. So big. The room was too warm. He felt so alone.

Unprotected. Unsafe.

*Snap out of it*, he told himself, irritated. The bed was fine. The room was fine. He wasn't alone. He was fine.

He wasn't fine.

He was trembling. He knew rationally that he was safe, that he wasn't in that cellar anymore, but his heart was beating too fast, his palms sweaty.

He wanted Damiano.

He wanted to sleep with Damiano. Wanted to smell him, to hear his voice. To have him on top of him, feel the reassuring weight of his muscular body crushing him, making him feel safe. Everything in him *ached* for it, for his closeness.

Jordan had no idea how much time passed before he finally lost the battle with himself.

He got out of the bed and left the room, his bare feet padding on the cold marble floor.

The corridor was dark. And narrow. Was it always so narrow or was he imagining it? Fuck, he hated this. Hated how shaky and unsure he felt. This wasn't him. He was a grown, competent, self-assured man, not this mess.

But all the self-hatred and mortification in his gut weren't enough to make him return to his room.

He had only a vague idea about the location of Damiano's room, but the villa wasn't enormous or anything: there were probably just ten bedrooms on this floor and apparently most of the family had already left.

He found the right bedroom on his fourth attempt. He knew it was the right one from the moment he stepped into it. It smelled right. Not that it had a strong smell or anything—not at all. But something about the combination of man and expensive cologne reminded him of how Damiano smelled the first day of their captivity, before the waterboarding.

The scent alone made something inside him ease.

Jordan walked toward the bed and stared at the man sleeping in it.

It was pretty dark. The room was illuminated only by the pale moonlight. But he would've recognized this man half-blind, the shape of him, the way the shadows seemed to envelop him gently, accentuating his sharp, angular features and strong, clean-shaven jaw.

Rationally, Jordan knew that this was a very dangerous, cold-hearted man. But he felt like safety to him, no matter how irrational it was.

Damiano was lying on his side, his bare chest rising and falling rhythmically. Jordan could see that the bruises on his ribs had been treated, and when he stepped closer and craned his neck, he saw that Damiano's back had some kind of bandages.

Thank fuck. At least he'd gotten medical help somewhere. Jordan tried to ignore the crazy, idiotic part of him that wondered obsessively who Damiano had trusted enough to reveal his weakened state to. *Who, who, who?*

Quashing those bizarre, ridiculous thoughts, Jordan climbed into the bed and stretched out, facing Damiano.

He breathed deeply, his muscles relaxing and all the remaining anxiety leaving his body.

Damiano murmured something in Italian and threw his arm over Jordan, hauling him close and stretching half on top of him in his customary position. Jordan smiled sleepily, feeling a rush of unbearable affection. For a man who didn't cuddle Damiano sure had his favorite way of doing so.

He was still smiling as he fell asleep, feeling perfectly content with the world.

He wasn't sure what woke him up. The comforting feeling of being crushed under Damiano's weight was still there, and he felt safe and marvelous and sleepy, but…

He could feel someone watching him.

Jordan opened his eyes blearily and made a questioning sound.

"What are you doing here?" Damiano said.

Yawning, Jordan peered at him. The room was brighter, so it was probably around dawn, and he could see Damiano's face fairly well.

Not that it helped him read him: his face was absolutely blank, only his eyes watching Jordan intently.

"I…" Jordan licked his lips, feeling awake enough to feel awkward. "I can go if you don't want me here."

Damiano didn't move, still watching him like a hawk. "How long have you been here?" he said, and there was something like bemusement in his voice now.

"I have no idea," Jordan said, rubbing at his eyes. "Probably three, four hours? Maybe more?"

Damiano's expression became faintly pinched. "Impossible. I sleep light. I should have woken up the moment you approached the bed, much less…" He looked at the way their bodies were entangled with a tight look in his eyes.

Jordan reached up and stroked his dark hair gently. It was so soft and thick when it was clean. "You must have gotten so used to sleeping with me that your body subconsciously didn't consider me a threat."

Damiano didn't exactly look reassured by that. "You can't be here," he bit off, even though he was leaning into the touch. "Why are you here?"

"Do you want me to go?" Jordan said, feeling a rush of fondness mixed with amusement.

It was like petting a wild, dangerous cat that leaned into his touch even as it bared its teeth at him menacingly.

"Why are you here?" Damiano said again, ignoring his question—or refusing to answer it.

Jordan buried his other hand in Damiano's hair. "I couldn't sleep without you," he answered with a rueful smile. "I guess you aren't the only one whose body got used to certain things."

Damiano's throat worked.

"Are you under the impression that this is what I do normally?" he said in a clipped voice. "I don't cuddle. Much less with my stepbrother's boyfriend."

Carding his fingers through his hair, Jordan murmured, "I don't do this normally, either. I'm not—I'm not this needy normally. The whole thing fucked us up. I'm sure it'll pass. We just need time."

Damiano's lips pressed together. He opened his mouth, staring at Jordan weirdly, but then closed it without saying anything. He sighed, tucking his face into the crook of Jordan's neck. "Fine. Just for tonight." A pause. "You're returning home soon, right?"

"Tomorrow," Jordan said, his stomach clenching at the thought. It *was* good. Being an ocean away sounded like a good way to get rid of this clinginess.

Damiano bit him on his neck, then sucked, and a small sound left Jordan's mouth.

*I adore you*, came an unbidden thought, his throat closing up from the intensity of the emotion. What the fuck. He couldn't adore him. He would go home tomorrow, and they would never see each other again, would go on with their lives an ocean apart. He hated the thought, and he hated the way it made him feel: panicky and desperate, as if he were back in the cellar without Damiano.

He didn't want to say goodbye, not like this, not yet. Jordan wanted—needed—more of him.

He pressed Damiano's face harder against his neck, silently asking for more bites. For more marks.

Damiano obliged, sucking hard all over his neck, his firm, hard body wonderfully heavy and grounding on top of him.

Jordan panted, feeling like he could expire from sheer pleasure and desperation. He'd never needed anyone this much. He roamed his greedy hands all over Damiano's hair, his shoulders, his smooth, muscular arms, hating that he couldn't touch his back, hating that he couldn't even hold him properly. He couldn't get enough. He wanted— he wanted… He wanted to take him inside his body, feel him on the deepest possible level.

"Let me suck your cock," he blurted out as he realized what he wanted. Taking a part of Damiano's body into his own, giving him pleasure, feeling him from the *inside*… it had a twisted, messed-up appeal that had nothing to do with him liking to suck cock on occasion. It wasn't about sex. He just needed him closer. Needed an outlet for the needy, messy feeling in his chest. "Give me your cock."

Damiano was very still on top of him, his body rigid with tension. "I'm not gay," he said after a moment, but Jordan could feel him twitch against his thigh, hardening.

"Who cares?" Jordan said, slipping his hand between them and palming Damiano's cock through his boxer-briefs before pulling it out. It was gratifyingly half-hard already and quickly grew to full hardness at his touch. "Maybe it'll help—fix us. Come on. Let me suck it."

Damiano was breathing harshly into his neck, his cock hot and throbbing in Jordan's hand.

"What about Raffaele?" he gritted out, his teeth sinking into his neck again. His voice became nasty as he said, "Your *boyfriend*?"

Jordan shivered, giving him better access. He hoped there would be marks.

"Don't want him. Want you."

Damiano let out an unsteady breath and didn't say anything for a while. Jordan was fine with it, stroking Damiano's cock and enjoying how warm, thick, and firm it was in his hand.

"Fine," Damiano said at last, sitting up. The corners of his mouth were tight, unhappy, as if his cock wasn't rock hard. "Get on the floor."

If it were any other man, Jordan would have told him to fuck off. On the few occasions he'd sucked cock, it was in the comfort of his marriage bed, with his wife giving him pointers and encouragement along the way. It had never been about the men. Male bodies or faces didn't do anything for him. He only liked cock. His fascination with cock was similar to his fascination with breasts: the bigger the better, and they felt good in his mouth, felt good to suck on. He'd never been attracted to anything attached to a cock. Jordan had never cared about *pleasing* the man the cock belonged to, much less obeying him. It had always been about his own fun, not the other man's.

But it wasn't just any other man.

Part of him despised how much he needed this, needed this cold-hearted man, wanted to please him, make him feel good, but maybe it was okay. It was just for tonight, so it was okay. Just for this one night, he could get on his knees in front of this man, ignore the cold marble against his knees, the discomfort and confusion, and let Damiano feed him his cock.

He moaned around it, trying to take it all, trying to get him as deep inside him as he could, embarrassingly eager in a way he'd never been about blowjobs. Damiano's fingers tightened in his hair to the point of pain.

Damiano was eerily quiet as he fucked Jordan's mouth, only the unsteadiness of his breathing betraying his pleasure. When Jordan looked up at him, he saw his gray eyes watching him, transfixed, as his cock pistoned in and out of Jordan's mouth.

Jordan let him, let him use him, just taking it, and loving every second of it. He loved the way his lips were stretched wide to accommodate the girth of Damiano's cock, the way the friction stimulated his sensitive mouth, the taste and the texture. He moaned around the cock, unable to get enough, wanting to milk it dry. He craved Damiano's come, he realized with baffled embarrassment. He wanted his stomach to be full of it, have proof of pleasing Damiano and making him feel good. The thought appealed to him immensely: to have Damiano's bodily fluids deep inside him. Like a branding. A branding only they would know about. A tiny part of Damiano inside his body, invisible but there.

Fuck, it was a good thing he was leaving tomorrow and he'd never see this man again.

But instead of comforting him, the thought only made him more desperate. He bobbed his head, roughly fucking his mouth on Damiano's leaking cock, hungry, so very hungry. *Come in me, come in me, come in me.*

A quiet groan finally left Damiano's lips as he thrust hard and came deep in his throat.

Jordan coughed but swallowed greedily, the craving in him finally satisfied. He was full of Damiano's come. He had given him pleasure.

Except when he lifted his half-drunk gaze back to him, Damiano didn't look like a man who had just been thoroughly pleasured. His face was stony and he was looking at Jordan like he was a moment away from pulling out his gun and shooting him.

Jordan blinked, unconcerned, and let the cock slip out of his mouth. "Damiano?" he said, leaning his cheek against Damiano's muscular thigh and breathing. His voice sounded absolutely wrecked. He didn't mind.

Damiano stared at him for a long moment.

"Get back in the bed," he said at last, fixing his gaze on the opposite wall. "It's still early."

Jordan did as he was told, stretching out on his back. He was hard, but there was no real urgency. It hadn't been about sex. It had been pure need, the craving to have this man inside him, and it had been satisfied. But now he wanted cuddles.

He got what he wanted: Damiano yanked his boxer-briefs up and lay down on top of him. He buried his face in Jordan's neck again and breathed, his breaths too deep to be natural.

Jordan closed his eyes, threading his fingers through Damiano's hair, and fell asleep.

# Chapter 17

A sudden jolt woke Jordan up.

For a moment, he felt disoriented, but then his sleepy gaze focused on the man standing by the bed, looking at them.

Raffaele Ferrara.

Flushing, Jordan scrambled into a sitting position. He looked sideways at Damiano, who was already seated, leaning back against the pillows in a manner that would have seemed lazy if it weren't for the hard glint in his eyes.

Oh, and the fact that there was a gun in his hand.

He wasn't aiming it at Ferrara, thank fuck, but it wasn't very reassuring, considering what a fast shot he was. Jordan had no idea where Damiano had even gotten the gun from so fast. Did he sleep with a gun under his pillow?

The thought made his stomach clench. It seemed he was really lucky that Damiano's subconscious had gotten used to him so much that his body didn't react when Jordan climbed into the bed.

"Get out," Damiano said, looking at Raffaele coldly. "You know how much I hate to have my sleep interrupted."

Ferrara's lips thinned. If the gun unnerved him, he didn't show it. "You have some nerve. I won't leave without him."

Damiano smiled, his gray eyes glinting with something ugly. "Are you saying you're jealous? Don't be a hypocrite, Raffaele. Should I tell your boyfriend about the fuck-toy you have on the side?"

Fuck.

Jordan exchanged a look with his boss, and quickly made a decision. There was no point in lying anymore. Ferrara might not believe him, but Jordan knew it wasn't Damiano who had been trying to kill him. There was no reason not to tell him the truth.

"All right, that's enough," he said, pulling the gun out of Damiano's hand. "Give me that."

Damiano shot him a sour look but let him take the gun. Ferrara stared at them like they both had grown seconds heads overnight. In any other circumstances, Jordan would have laughed. He'd never seen his unflappable boss look so confused.

"First of all, he isn't my boyfriend," Jordan said. "He's my boss. He paid me to take his boyfriend's place on this trip, because he was concerned for Nate's safety and we look similar enough." He held Damiano's gaze steadily. "My real name is Jordan. Jordan Gates. I couldn't tell you the truth until we knew for sure that you weren't behind the assassination attempts on Raffaele and Nate."

"We still *know* no such thing," Ferrara said with a sigh, but Jordan ignored him, his eyes only on Damiano.

There was a very strange expression on Damiano's face, but he couldn't quite read it. Jordan couldn't tell what he was feeling—if he was feeling anything at all.

At last, Damiano shifted his gaze from Jordan to Ferrara. "Did you really think it was me?" he said, his lips twisting in derision. "I had a higher opinion of your intelligence. If I wanted you dead, you'd be dead. Killing you is pointless for me. The only people that would benefit from your death are your blood relatives, who can actually inherit your property. I'm pretty sure it was Gustavo—he's the one who needed money the most—so you're welcome."

"You killed him?" Ferrara said, frowning.

Damiano blinked and glanced at Jordan.

His ears uncomfortably warm, Jordan shook his head slightly.

A muscle jumped in Damiano's jaw, something almost like confusion appearing in his eyes, but his face was blank when he looked back at Ferrara. "I can neither confirm nor deny it. I can only say that he won't bother anyone anymore." He gave his stepbrother a cold look. "Though, it's possible that the culprit is Paolo or Andrea. I hope you weren't harboring the delusion that they liked you. As soon as Marco died and couldn't protect you anymore, you were always going to be an easy source for inheritance. If I were you, I'd write a will and tell your dearest cousins that if you die, you're leaving everything to charity."

Ferrara stared at him searchingly for a moment before nodding. "Jordan, let's go. Our flight is in a few hours."

Damiano's shoulders tensed, but he didn't say anything. He wouldn't even look at him.

His stomach in knots, Jordan got out of the bed and followed his boss out of the room.

The door clicked shut after them.

Ferrara remained quiet as they walked toward their rooms. Jordan had trouble looking at him, but he forced himself to. He was a grown man, not a flustered teenager.

"I couldn't sleep," he said tersely, hoping he didn't sound as defensive as he felt.

Ferrara eyed him. "Get packed. We're leaving for the airport in an hour."

Jordan nodded and went to his room, unsure if he was glad that Ferrara had chosen not to comment on the elephant in the room or not. He would have almost welcomed a reprimand. Anything was better than the tight ball of anxiety and dread that curled in his stomach every time he thought of never seeing Damiano again.

Having finished packing, he trudged downstairs with his suitcase and sat down on the wooden bench outside.

It was a wonderfully sunny day. The birds were chirping, the bees were buzzing around the flowers, the scent of Italian air was as sweet as it had been upon their arrival.

It was a perfect day.

Jordan tried to feel the perfection of it, but the heavy feeling in his chest didn't leave room for anything else. He wasn't sure what the feeling was. He couldn't name it. It was a mix of sadness, regret, wistfulness, and *what-ifs*.

His heart jumped when there was the sound of footsteps. He turned his head and told himself he wasn't disappointed when he saw Ferrara approaching him with his suitcase.

Forcing a smile, Jordan got to his feet. "Ready to go?"

He wasn't sure why he bothered. Ferrara's dark eyes seemed to see right through him. But his boss didn't comment on it as they put their suitcases into the trunk of the car.

Jordan carefully didn't look back at the house as he got into the car. He didn't look in the rearview mirror, either. He knew him. He knew he wouldn't come out to say goodbye. Even if—*if*—he cared enough to do it, he wouldn't want people to see him caring about anyone. He perceived it as a weakness.

"I'm sorry for dragging you into this mess," Ferrara said stiffly as the car rolled away from the villa. He was looking out the window, giving Jordan a semblance of privacy as he put himself together.

"It's fine," Jordan said with a laugh. "I'm fine. I'm nearly two hundred thousand dollars richer. I have nothing to complain about."

He hated how fake his voice sounded. He hated how very far from fine he actually felt. Christ, it was so stupid. He'd known the guy for thirteen days. He shouldn't have been such a mess when he couldn't even define what Damiano had become to him. Someone not quite a friend and not quite a lover. Someone he loathed, needed, and adored. Someone he understood on an intimate level and didn't understand at all. Someone who, in different circumstances, in another life, might have become more.

But *might have, could have* didn't matter.

His real life waited for him in the U.S.

And there was no place for Damiano Conte in it.

# Chapter 18

Jordan had always been good at compartmentalizing his emotions.

That skill now helped him adjust back to his life in Boston. Overall, it was pretty seamless. He went to work, and he was as efficient at his job as ever. He went to his gym on weekends, to work out and box. He ran every morning before work. Every few weeks, he met up with his friends and visited his parents. On the surface, his life was exactly like his life before the trip to Italy.

What happened below the surface was another matter entirely.

He knew he was still a mess, and to his frustration, he wasn't getting better. He couldn't use elevators at all, his claustrophobia worse than it had ever been. He had to keep the door to the bathroom open when he showered. He flinched at every sudden noise. He hated being alone in the dark. He slept only with the lights on.

Not that he was sleeping much. He tossed and turned in bed for hours, staring at the ceiling and longing for a hard body on top of him. It got so bad that he tried to sleep with pillows on top of him, to trick his mind and give himself the pressure he craved. It didn't work. He was lucky to get some decent sleep once in five nights, when he was too exhausted to crave anything.

Lack of sleep didn't exactly help his overall mental state. He was cranky, jumpy, and more snappish at work. He'd never exactly been beloved by his subordinates, but now they grew quiet and wary every time he walked past their cubicles.

After one month of this hell, Jordan finally took Ferrara up on his offer and let him pay for the services of a therapist.

He deeply regretted it after the very first session. He didn't want to talk about his *feelings*. He didn't want to talk about Damiano. He didn't need a therapist to know how messed-up the whole thing was. He wasn't an idiot.

But at least the therapist had given him a prescription for sleeping pills to turn his brain off and finally get some sleep. He hated how the pills made him feel: groggy, weak, and somehow even more anxious, but they were the only solution for his insomnia. Jordan tried not to use them too often, not wanting to become dependent on yet another thing, but sometimes it was necessary.

Thankfully, there was some good news too. His landlord offered him an apartment on the third floor once he heard of Jordan's inability to use elevators. The apartment was twice as large as his old one, which hadn't been small either, but to his surprise, his landlord didn't charge him more. Maybe he felt sorry for him.

Either way, Jordan decided not to look a gift horse in the mouth. This building was really good, and he had been dreading the necessity of looking for another apartment on a lower floor. It was good to see some things going his way for once.

But his good mood after the move didn't last. The new apartment was completely unfamiliar (*unsafe*) and only made his discomfort and anxiety worse.

He couldn't stay inside it for a long time, the walls closing in on him no matter how spacious the rooms were.

That was how Jordan ended up spending a lot of time outside. He started going for long walks in the evening after work. It made breathing a little easier. And it helped him sleep, a little.

Jordan was walking home through the park that evening when some drunks decided that they had nothing better to do than bother him.

At first Jordan ignored them. He knew the type: a bunch of frat boys, high on alcohol, weed, and their own self-importance, just messing around on a Friday evening, trying to get some tail. If he ignored them and continued walking, they'd leave him alone.

Except they didn't leave him alone.

"You think you're too good for us or something?" one of them growled, grabbing his shoulder and forcing him to stop.

Jordan sighed inwardly. He wasn't worried. He could handle himself against three drunks. But he really didn't feel like breaking his knuckles against those dickheads' jaws.

But before he could do anything, two burly men in dark clothes materialized seemingly out of nowhere. "Get lost," one of them said, staring the drunks down. He let his jacket fall open, revealing a gun in his holster.

"Okaaay, dude, whatever," the frat boy said, letting go of Jordan and stepping back. His friends dragged him away.

Jordan frowned and turned back to the men who'd come to his aid, but they weren't there anymore. Jordan stared at the empty space they had just been in, his stomach tightening and his heart beating faster.

No.

Surely not.

He wouldn't do that.

But those men… they seemed like professionals. Normal people wouldn't slip back into the shadows after helping out someone. They'd say something, wait for thanks. Not just disappear.

Jordan looked around, but the park was dark and quiet. If there were people watching him—following him—they were very, very good.

If.

He *could* be wrong.

His pulse beating fast in his throat, Jordan continued walking. He couldn't see or hear people following him. Everything seemed normal.

After a while, he started feeling ridiculous. Maybe he'd imagined the weirdness. Maybe he'd been saved by passersby.

And maybe pigs flew.

*Think, Gates,* he told himself, pushing his messy emotions into a box. *What are the chances of two random men with guns materializing out of nowhere when you need help and then disappearing as soon as you turn around? Extremely slim.*

All right.

He could test it.

Every theory should be tested.

Jordan considered his options. The test shouldn't be done with the same variables. If there were people following him around, he couldn't let them know that he was aware of it.

So he strolled forward, without looking around. He pulled his phone out and started browsing his messages, pretending to be completely unaware of his surroundings.

He was a block away from his apartment when he decided to act.

Pretending to be engrossed in his phone, he stopped in the middle of the street just as a car came around the corner. The car was coming with too much speed, and the driver honked frantically, but Jordan pretended to be too distracted to hear. *Come on, come on, come on.*

Just as he was about to give up—no test was worth his life—someone grabbed his arm and yanked him back.

He quickly turned, his heart in his throat, and found the same guy from before trying to disappear into the crowd.

Well, fuck.

*** 

He couldn't sleep that night. That was nothing unusual, but this time the reason was different. He was shaking with a horrible mix of toxic anger and irrational excitement. He told himself the anger was the prevailing emotion. Who did Damiano think he was, putting bodyguards on him without asking Jordan's opinion when the asshole hadn't even bothered to come out to say goodbye to him? Arrogant, overbearing dick.

*(God, he missed him.)*

Jesus. It pissed him off that the mere possibility of being followed—stalked—by Damiano's people pleased a part of him. *It means that he cares,* said a small, stupid voice at the back of his mind, like a little girl hugging her favorite toy to her chest and refusing to see that the toy was a demon, not a cute plushie.

The grown-ass adult that Jordan was *wasn't* impressed.

He would never move on with his life if Damiano had him shadowed and was still constantly on his mind. It had to stop.

He might not be able to control his thoughts and fixation, but the unwanted bodyguarding was something he could control. Hopefully.

The problem was, he didn't have Damiano's number or any other way of contacting him.

Except…

Jordan smiled grimly.

***

He pretended to trip and fall during his morning run. Pretending to have hit his head and fainted, Jordan lay still and waited.

Soon enough, there were the sounds of footsteps and voices.

"Should we call 911?" a guy said, his voice full of doubt. "We aren't supposed to be seen by him."

"Fuck, why did it have to happen during our shift?" the other guy grumbled, sighing.

"This gig fucking sucks," the first man said. "I still don't get why we're babysitting this guy. It's so random. He's not interesting at all."

Jordan tried not to take offense. By gangsters' standards, he probably *was* very boring.

"At least the money is good."

One of them nudged him with his shoe. "Hey, you. Wake up."

"Let's just call 911. What if he dies? The boss said this gig is important, comes from somewhere very high up."

"Do you know who?"

"Nah, no idea. But between you and me, the boss seemed scared shitless. He stressed several times that a failure isn't acceptable. Just call 911 before he dies."

Figuring he wouldn't learn more than that, Jordan turned onto his back and sat up.

The two men—they weren't the same men from yesterday—flinched and exchanged a look.

"You okay?" one of them said, clearly hoping to pass for a random passerby. "Saw you trip and fall."

Jordan pulled out the envelope he'd prepared beforehand and smiled. "I'm fine. But you guys wouldn't mind passing this to your boss's boss?"

He pretended not to notice the nervous look they exchanged. He paused, thinking. He doubted Damiano personally dealt with these guys' boss. "Or maybe even to your boss's boss's boss. Basically, pass this to the man who hired you to 'babysit' me." His smile turned sweeter when they paled. "Be fast, and no peeking. You wouldn't want to upset the guy who has your boss scared shitless, right?"

After a moment that seemed to stretch forever, one of the men finally spoke.

"All right," he said, taking the envelope carefully, as if it were poisonous. "We'll pass it along."

Jordan smiled. "Thanks. Carry on."

They disappeared so fast Jordan felt a pang of admiration. For such big guys, they were really fast. At least Damiano hadn't hired incompetents.

He wondered how long it would take before the message reached Damiano. Knowing Damiano's general paranoia, it would probably pass through the hands of at least four middlemen before reaching him. Jordan had little doubt it would be read by someone along the way, but he wasn't worried. He hadn't written anything incriminating.

The message just said,
*Stop*.

# Chapter 19

If Jordan were honest with himself, he didn't really think his message would make Damiano stop.

If he were even more honest with himself, sending that little message made him feel more normal than he'd felt in months. That little message was a connection to something he'd hungered for against his better judgment. No matter how small, it made him feel better, his mind sharper and less of a mess.

Days passed.

Then a week.

And yet nothing happened. If he was still being followed around, his new bodyguards were very good at staying hidden.

Could it be possible that Damiano had actually listened to his request?

It pissed Jordan off that he was sulking over it, instead of being pleased. He was behaving like a teenager with his first crush, instead of the grown, successful man he was. And over whom? A *man*, when he wasn't even bi! The whole thing was so ridiculous Jordan wanted to laugh at himself—if he hadn't felt like punching something.

He returned home that evening in a shitty mood. It was the sort of day when everything that could go wrong went wrong: after yet another sleepless night, he'd fallen asleep at dawn and overslept, there hadn't been time to have breakfast, so he was hungry and cranky without his morning coffee; Ferrara had been more of a bastard than usual and given his department an impossible deadline; Jordan's secretary told him that she was quitting; someone had accidentally locked up Jordan in a restroom and he'd had a massive panic attack, and then had to pretend that he was fine because he was at work and people expected nothing short of perfection from him.

By the time Jordan arrived home, he felt like crawling into his bed and never leaving it.

Except when he unlocked his door, there was light in his living room.

And there was a tall, dark-haired man standing by the open window, smoking out of it.

Jordan's heart jumped somewhere to his throat. He dropped his briefcase with a thud and shut the door with shaking hands. His whole body was taut as a bowstring, his nails digging deep crescents into his palms. "Didn't I tell you not to smoke indoors?"

The man turned, the cigarette between his long fingers.

"I opened the window," Damiano said, his gray eyes giving nothing away.

*Smoking is bad for you,* Jordan nearly said. He had to bite his tongue. Damiano wasn't his to fret over. He was no one to him.

"Aren't you afraid someone might shoot you while you stand there? You probably make a very easy target."

Damiano took a long drag from his cigarette. He looked mouthwateringly attractive, his sharp, angular face so striking it made Jordan's fingers itch to draw him or take a picture.

Distantly, Jordan was exasperated with himself. Why this man? If he had to find a man attractive, why did it have to be this one? The worst possible choice?

"I bought the building opposite this one," Damiano said. "It's secure now."

Jordan looked at the skyscraper visible in the window and nearly laughed. "Right. Of course you did." Shaking his head, he loosened his tie and pulled it off. "Look, I've had a spectacularly shitty day. Just tell me why you're here and go. I have a hot date with my pillow I really don't want to miss."

Damiano eyed him for a moment before stubbing his cigarette out on the windowsill. "You look terrible, *caro*."

Something lodged in his throat. "Thanks."

"You haven't slept in days," Damiano stated, walking toward him and stopping just a few inches away.

Jordan's heart was attempting to escape from his chest, or at least it felt like it. He shoved his hands into the pockets of his suit jacket, so that he couldn't reach out for this man greedily. He wanted to reach out and touch, trace his stubbled jawline, his neck, his everything. He wanted to taste his skin, hot and salty, smell his sweat.

"Don't tell me you have people stalking me in my sleep and reporting to you how much sleep I get," Jordan said with as much bite as he could manage. It wasn't a lot. His body was instinctively leaning forward, *needing*, and it was maddeningly difficult not to just fall into this man and cling to him with all his strength.

"I don't need to have you stalked for that," Damiano said, his nostrils flaring as his eyes roamed all over Jordan's face. "You do look terrible. Too pale. Sickly. Almost plain."

"Oh, wow," Jordan said with a laugh. "You sure know how to make a guy feel special."

Damiano's face did something strange: a tight, pinched look, his eyes all pissy and angry, before he stepped forward and *shoved* his face into Jordan's neck.

The punched-out noise that left Jordan's mouth didn't even sound like him, his eyes closing and his hands gripping, roaming all over Damiano's back greedily before burying in his thick, gorgeous hair. It was like the rest of the world simply faded into nothing, put on mute or something.

Teeth bit him on his neck so hard Jordan cried out from the familiar, exquisite pain-pleasure. "Easy there, asshole," he gasped out, clutching him close, clinging to his firm, sturdy body, trying to tug him tighter, closer. The fabric separating their skin pissed him off, so he yanked at Damiano's shirt, buttons flying everywhere. Finally, the stupid thing was off and there was so much skin he could touch: warm, glorious skin covering the familiar, smooth muscles.

Damiano ignored his words, sucking nasty hickeys all over his neck, his confident hands making quick work of the buttons of Jordan's shirt. Jordan was shaking, whines leaving his mouth—such an embarrassing sound, but he couldn't seem to stop, needing him so fucking badly. He wanted to be naked with him. He wanted to be *fused* to him, like conjoined twins.

They stumbled into Jordan's bed half-naked already, and Jordan moaned in delight as Damiano pressed him into it with his body, his weight so familiar, comforting, and achingly good. It felt so right: the weight, the pressure, the smell, the *man*. He missed this so badly.

His cock was hard, Jordan realized distantly. In any other circumstances, with a different man, it would have surprised him. But of course his cock was hard now.

He craved this man with every cell of his body. Of course it would manifest as a physical want, too. It didn't even feel all that strange to him. If there was a man who could make him want, it was this one. The mere thought of being naked with Damiano and feeling all of his skin against his own made him shiver, his nipples tingling. He wanted it.
He wanted him so badly. He wanted to eat Damiano alive, swallow him whole, consume him in ways that weren't even possible.

As if sensing his needs, Damiano moved his head lower, his hot mouth sucking hard hickeys down his neck, his pec, before biting the hard nipple. Jordan moaned, and then moaned louder when Damiano pressed his tongue against it, licking the nipple lewdly, and then *sucking*. Jordan nearly came, right there.

He wrapped his legs around Damiano, seeking friction, some relief for his stiff, aching cock. He could feel Damiano's erection against his thigh, and it gave him such a rush. *He* made it happen. Damiano was hard for him. He needed to see his cock. He needed to touch it. He needed it in his mouth.

Jordan fumbled between them, trying to get Damiano's belt open and failing—his fingers were shaking too badly.

The other man huffed and, knocking his hands away, made quick work of his belt and zipper. "Get naked," Damiano commanded.

After much fumbling, Jordan got naked, somehow. The whole thing was complicated by his inability to be parted from Damiano even for a few seconds, their bodies grinding even as they undressed.

Finally, they both were naked, and it felt beyond glorious, to feel so much skin. Jordan's head was spinning and he was making low, shameless noises as he clung to the man on top of him. They rutted together like animals, Damiano's teeth in his neck, his body heavy and perfect on top of him. There was no rhythm or finesse to it, it was every man for himself, seeking release from the maddening tension. There, almost there—

Damiano suddenly shoved Jordan's thighs upward, pressing them together to create friction for his cock between them. God, Damiano was fucking his thighs, using him as a cock-sleeve to get off. It should have felt humiliating or mortifying, but all it did was turn Jordan on. He clung to Damiano's back with hitching mewls, feeling powerful muscle ripple underneath smooth skin with the rolling rhythm of Damiano's hips fucking his thighs, the bed creaking ominously, but not loud enough to mask Jordan's moans. So good—so fucking good…

Jordan grabbed his own weeping cock and jacked off, fast and needy, and much too soon, he was coming all over his hand with a sob.

Damiano fucked him through his orgasm, though his own, each buck messier and shakier than the last until he finally went boneless on top of him, breathing hard, his weight crushing. Jordan couldn't breathe under him, but he didn't care. It was perfect. Everything was perfect. Even the mess on his thighs felt perfect. He was covered in Damiano's come. As it should be.

As it should be.

And yet.

It still wasn't enough. It was so weird. Although he felt physically spent after his orgasm, Jordan still didn't feel satisfied, somehow still wanting more. He ran greedy hands over the expanse of Damiano's back, reveling in smooth skin and muscle.

"You don't have scars," he murmured. "I thought there would be scars for sure."

"There were," Damiano said into his neck. "I've had them removed."

Jordan considered joking about his vanity, but he knew it wasn't really about vanity at all. It was about the illusion of infallible strength. Scars would show that Damiano had been vulnerable. Weak.

This man couldn't afford to have weaknesses. Any weaknesses.

"You should go," Jordan said, looking at the ceiling.

"Yes," Damiano said, sucking on the tender bruise on his neck.

Jordan bit the inside of his cheek to stop himself from making any embarrassing noises. "Stop that. I can't go to work looking like I've been mauled by a vampire. I'm a department head. People are supposed to respect me."

"A few bruises won't make them respect you less," Damiano said, but he did stop nibbling on his neck and lifted himself on an elbow to look down at him.

Jordan felt his chest tighten as their gazes met. "You shouldn't have come."

"You shouldn't have sent for me, then."

Jordan glared at him. "I didn't—"

"Let's cut the bullshit, *caro*," Damiano said, his tone mild but his gaze almost resentful. "We both know your little message was a cry for attention. You knew I wouldn't ignore it. You knew I'd come to see you."

Jordan's face was burning with humiliation. "You didn't have to come. I hardly forced you."

The laugh that left Damiano's throat lacked true mirth. "I had no more agency than a moth that flies to a flame."

Right. How was he supposed to take that?

"I didn't make you put your guard dogs on me," Jordan ground out.

Damiano averted his gaze. "That was just a precaution. I wanted to make sure you didn't become someone of interest."

Jordan laughed. "Yeah, and putting bodyguards on me 24/7 didn't make me someone of interest. Great logic." He buried his fingers in Damiano's hair and yanked slightly, forcing him to look at him. "As you say, let's cut the bullshit. You did it because you're an emotionally stunted control freak who got a little bit attached and doesn't know how to express his affections in a healthy way."

"I've killed people for less," Damiano said, his tone very mild but his expression tight.

Chuckling, Jordan pulled his head down and pecked him on the stubbled cheek. "Is that supposed to intimidate me? You never scared me."

Damiano inhaled unsteadily. "Why didn't you tell Raffaele that I killed Gustavo?"

Jordan licked his lips. There were so many ways to answer that question.

But he couldn't lie. Not to this man.

"You know why," he said, closing his eyes.

"Say it," Damiano said hoarsely, his teeth grazing Jordan's jawline.

Jordan shivered. *More.*

"He paid me $180,000 to pretend to be his boyfriend and help him figure out who was behind the assassination attempts. I did what he paid me for. I owed him nothing more. Loyalty can't be bought. And mine belonged to you, not him."

Damiano kissed his neck, his hand gripping Jordan's side almost painfully. "You're smarter than that. No one trusts me, *caro*."

"I do." The terrifying part was how little he cared about Damiano's faults. He'd always considered himself a pretty good person, but lately he had to reevaluate that opinion. A good person wouldn't adore a man who was capable of killing in cold blood—who had killed someone in front of him.

Damiano pressed their foreheads together, his breath warm against Jordan's cheek.

He didn't say anything for a long time, breathing unsteadily.

"I can't stand this," he said at last, his voice barely audible. "I hate the way you got me all twisted up and irrational. This is not me." He sucked hard on Jordan's jawline. "You're right: giving you bodyguards was irrational. But it was something I could control. Knowing how you're doing. It helped, a little."

Jordan's eyes burned. God, they both were so fucked-up.

He hugged Damiano tightly, pulling his weight fully on top of him again. He loved it, he hated it, he hated this feeling so much. How could something feel so good, so perfect, and yet leave him feeling so empty? Missing someone who had never been his, who was still right there, was its own special kind of hell.

"Stay," he said in a disgustingly small voice. "Just for tonight?"

It seemed to take ages before Damiano replied.

"All right." He put his head on Jordan's pillow, his body still on top of him and their faces inches apart.

His throat uncomfortably tight, Jordan traced

Damiano's features with a finger, trying to imprint them into memory.

Damiano allowed him, just watching him with an intense, fixated expression, the intimacy of the moment gut-wrenching. He'd never felt closer to another person in his life. He'd never wanted to be even closer. Was there a way to be closer? If there was, Jordan wanted it. He couldn't get enough. He would bottle up this man's scent if he could. He would spend the rest of his life in this bed with him if he could.

But he couldn't.

He knew Damiano wouldn't return. He wasn't the sort of man to indulge his weaknesses. He would quash any unwanted emotions until there was nothing left.

This was the last time he'd ever see him.

"Don't cry," Damiano said tersely, a muscle jumping by his temple. "It's not worth crying over."

*I'm not worth crying over.*

"I'm not crying," Jordan said, blinking the moisture away.

Damiano cradled his cheek carefully, wiping the tear by the corner of Jordan's right eye with the pad of his thumb, his touch ever so gentle. The gentleness of it made Jordan's throat close up.

Damiano stared at the tear in strange fascination as if he'd never seen tears in his life. "Our paths should have never crossed," he said tonelessly. "Whatever this is, it'll pass. You'll be better off without me."

"I know," Jordan whispered. He closed his eyes, pressing his cheek against Damiano's.

*Stay,* he wanted to beg. It was his last thought as he drifted off. *Stay.*

It was the best sleep he'd gotten in months.

When he woke up, the bed was empty.

Damiano had slipped out of his bed and his life like he had never been in it.

# Chapter 20

The ironic thing was, Damiano utterly detested stalking.

He saw nothing wrong with gathering vital intelligence about people of interest when it came to business, but stalking a person just for the sake of it… he'd always thought it was pathetic. Only weak, pathetic men wouldn't approach the object of their interest instead of stalking them from afar. That had always been his opinion on the matter, and it generally irritated him if one of his men used their resources to stalk people for private reasons.

And yet here he was.

Stalking Jordan. Using his infinite resources to keep tabs on him, because—

Because he couldn't let go. Because part of him felt *entitled* to it. It was disgusting, how entitled to it he felt. How possessive his thoughts turned when he thought about Jordan.

Possessiveness wasn't exactly a new thing for Damiano. As a boy, he'd had very little. He had often felt like a changeling, an outsider among a big, tightly knit family, and he always had to fight to keep his place there. What little he owned, he had guarded fiercely from the other boys, afraid that they'd take it away.

As a boy, he had resolved to get stronger so that his things wouldn't be taken from him again. And he had gotten stronger. Rich. Respected. Feared. Along the way, he'd lost his fierce desire to own things and guard them. He had everything now. Why would he be possessive of his things if he could just buy another?

He'd forgotten how ugly, how fierce his possessiveness could be. It listened to no reason. He felt entitled to watch Jordan, no matter how much his rational side was disgusted and irritated with the situation—with his own weakness.

No matter what he told himself, Damiano still found himself watching the live feed every night before bed. He watched for a couple of minutes, to make sure that Jordan was fine, and then turned the video off, the deep, gnawing pit in his chest a little placated. Placated, but never satisfied. It was beyond aggravating, but Damiano had gotten used to the feeling over the past months.

The only time the need was remotely sated was when he had literally put part of his body inside Jordan—when Jordan had sucked his cock—but that was something he'd tried not to think about, the memory making him uneasy.

His unease had nothing to do with Jordan being a man. Damiano had always considered himself straight, but he also wasn't bothered by the idea of gay sex. Normally, what he wanted, he took. If it happened to be a man, it wouldn't make much of a difference. But Jordan wasn't just someone he wanted to stick his cock into. It would have been simpler if he were. Damiano would have just fucked him and moved on.

The problem was, his desire to fuck Jordan didn't really stem from his cock. It was a twisted, insane desire to *possess*, a desire for closeness and ownership that happened to affect his cock too. He wanted to devour him, to tear into his heart and burrow his way inside. Even during his last visit, the rush he got from coming all over Jordan's thighs had little to do with physical pleasure and everything to do with his desire to own him, to mark him up, to brand him as his. He felt like a dog that wanted to piss all over his territory. It was utterly disgusting—and utterly dangerous.

Sighing, Damiano sat down in his bed and opened his laptop. A few clicks, and he was watching the live feed from Jordan's apartment.

But this time it wasn't Jordan he saw on screen.

Not just Jordan.

Damiano went rigid as he stared at the video before enlarging it.

There was a man sitting next to Jordan on the couch in the living room. They were sitting way too close, both of them nursing beers as they talked. The stranger was smirking in an obnoxiously flirtatious way, the way men did when they were hoping to get laid soon.

Jordan was harder to read, his body language stiff, but he was smiling and he didn't pull back when the other man put his hand on his thigh in a rather possessive manner.

Something ugly twisted up Damiano's insides. There was a creak of plastic and, glancing down, he realized he was holding the laptop too tightly. His knuckles were white.

*Mine*, the thing inside him said. *Mineminemine.*

He tried to quash it, but it was fruitless. He could barely think as he reached for his phone and found Jordan's number.

He pressed Call before he could stop himself.

He watched Jordan flinch as his phone went off. Jordan looked at the screen and his face went very still.

Jordan didn't have his number, of course. But the Italian country code would probably give him an idea of who might be calling him.

He didn't wonder if Jordan would answer. He knew he would.

Jordan's throat worked before he walked away from that dickhead and brought his phone to his ear.

"Don't tell me you have my apartment bugged, you creep," he hissed.

"Tell him to leave," Damiano said. "And to never come back."

Jordan huffed. "You're unbelievable."

"Throw him out," he said softly. "I will give you the attention you so badly wanted from me."

It was just a guess, but it was gratifying to be confirmed correct when Jordan's pale face flushed.

"Fuck off," Jordan said, but he did turn to the dickhead and say something. There was no sound in the video, because Damiano normally had it turned off.

"Happy?" Jordan said bitingly when the guy left, but his tone didn't match his expression. There was some irritation there, but it wasn't the strongest emotion.

"What happened to you being straight?" Damiano said.

"None of your business," Jordan said, stretching out on the couch and putting his head on a throw pillow. He looked tired and soft with his hair rumpled. "But if you must know, I was horny and worked up, and that guy was just there. I figured I might as well let him suck my cock."

"And him looking like a poor man's version of me is pure coincidence?"

Jordan turned onto his back and glared at the ceiling. "Shut up," he grumbled without much heat. His jaw worked, his lovely blue eyes darting around the room. "Where is the camera?"

"To your left. High on the shelf above the TV, I think."

Jordan turned his head, squinting at the camera. "It must be really tiny, because I still don't see it."

"You're looking right at it."

"Huh." Jordan didn't attempt to get to his feet and remove the camera. He just stared at it for a long while before saying in a dejected voice, "It pisses me off that your creepy stalking doesn't even piss me off."

"That's ironic, because my creepy stalking does piss me off," Damiano said, his gaze roaming over Jordan's face. He liked looking at him. He hated just how much he liked looking at him. How could a person's face become a source of comfort after ten days of sleeping on top of the other man—literally—and looking after each other? It made no fucking sense. Or maybe it did make sense on a base, instinctive level, but it wasn't a good enough explanation for Damiano.

This wasn't him.

He wanted to stop feeling this way. Jordan muddled his thoughts, made him irrational. Reckless. Stupidly obsessive. Stupidly obsessed. Just plain stupid.

"Then stop stalking me," Jordan said.

"Thanks for the advice," Damiano ground out. "I would if I could."

That was the crux of the problem. He couldn't stop. His self-control and rational thinking went out the window when it came to this man.

Jordan's throat worked. Sighing, he closed his eyes.

"I'm still horny," he said with no self-consciousness whatsoever. But then again, they'd seen each other at their worst and weakest. Admitting horniness was nothing.

"And you're telling me that why?" Damiano said.

"Well, you did chase off my booty call, so it's your fault."

"I didn't chase him off. You did."

"You know what I mean, you ass." Jordan's expression was sour. "As if I could say no to you."

Christ.

Damiano stared at the ceiling, trying to ignore his thickening cock. This was a wrong thing to get aroused over.

He heard Jordan sigh again and murmur, "Do you know there are over four thousand miles from Boston to Italy?"

It seemed like a non sequitur, but Damiano knew it wasn't.

Silence fell over the line.

"You should jerk off," Damiano said, his voice more clipped than he would have liked. "I promise not to watch."

Jordan opened his eyes and looked straight at the camera, his expression strange. He licked his lips. "What if I want you to watch?"

Damiano went still, his stomach tightening and his cock twitching again. "Didn't know exhibitionism was your thing."

"It isn't," Jordan said with a bitter smile. "I just want—you know."

"I know," Damiano said. If Gustavo were still alive, Damiano wouldn't grant him a quick, painless death this time.

He would make him suffer for fucking them up like this.

"Go ahead, *caro*," he said, involuntarily adopting a gentler tone. Christ, he was disgustingly soft when it came to this man.

He watched Jordan unzip his fly and pull out his stiff cock. Jordan's breathing hitched in his throat, his eyes growing half-lidded and his cheeks slightly flushed. He put his phone on speaker. "Talk to me," he asked, stroking himself. "About anything. In Italian, if you want to. I just need to hear your voice."

Damiano pressed the heel of his hand to his cock and started talking in Italian, quietly recounting the events of the day, everything that had frustrated him about it. It felt freeing, and not just because Jordan didn't understand Italian. He *wanted* to tell him these things, share his thoughts with him and hear Jordan's opinion. Thankfully, he had enough self-control left to speak in Italian. It was risky to do even in Italian, no matter how secure the line was.

He hadn't even noticed when he pulled his cock out and started jerking off too, staring at Jordan's flushed face. It was strange. He was very much aroused, but it wasn't really about getting off. He wanted. He wanted to step into the screen, crawl on top of Jordan, put himself inside him, and *merge* them together.

The thought made him come, his orgasm catching him completely off-guard.

Damiano gritted his teeth and glared at the mess on his shirt, frustrated beyond belief despite the orgasm.

Christ. This was getting out of hand.

***

He told himself he wouldn't do it again.

He told himself he had better things to do with his time than to have weird sort-of phone sex with another man. He did have better things to do. Far more productive things.

But there were upsides of being the boss: no one could question him if he decided to set work aside and do something unproductive. The same thing was also the downside: that he didn't have anyone to answer to.

So he kept doing it.

And things got progressively weirder each time.

The second time it happened, Jordan was already in bed, so it didn't seem all that strange to ask him to get completely naked and let Damiano look at him.

"This is pretty weird, you know," Jordan said, but he didn't refuse, undressing without a hint of shame.

He had nothing to be ashamed of: he was a fit man with a toned, well-proportioned body. His legs were long and well-shaped for a man, his skin smooth and flawless, his torso hairless but for the trail of blond hair leading to his sizable cock. Objectively, he was a very handsome guy. A hot guy, even.

But it wasn't his body that made Damiano's cock fill out. At least, not just his body. Jordan's body didn't repel him or anything: Damiano could appreciate it aesthetically and he really liked the soft, vulnerable spot between Jordan's neck and shoulder, and those pink nipples, and his shapely, strong thighs. But Jordan was still a man, with a hard cock and balls instead of a pussy, and men normally didn't turn him on.

Jordan did, for all the wrong reasons.

Looking at Jordan's naked body gave him such a possessive thrill, all that skin on display at *his* request. Jordan was straight, but he had undressed for another man and let him ogle him because it was Damiano. Just for him. It was a power trip that really messed with his head and fed the possessive beast that lived under his skin. He wanted to know every curve and angle of Jordan's body, every hollow, every mole, every scar. It was his, he had a right to know that.

"Now open the package I sent you," Damiano said.

"Now?" Jordan grumbled, reluctantly taking his hand off his cock. But he did as he was told. Because he couldn't say no to him.

The thought made Damiano's cock ache, and he tugged at it absently, watching as Jordan unwrapped the package Damiano had sent via express courier delivery that morning.

"It's a shirt," Jordan said, blinking at the box's contents in confusion.

"It's mine."

It was incredibly satisfying to see Jordan's indifferent expression change to one of hunger.

Jordan pulled the shirt out and brought it to his face close enough to sniff it.

"It does smell like you," he said breathlessly, his face a little flushed.

"Put it on," Damiano ordered, his voice gone hoarse.

Jordan didn't put it on. He pressed it against his face and inhaled audibly, his eyes becoming unfocused.

Jesus fucking Christ.

Damiano stroked his cock harder, watching Jordan breathe in his scent like it was his favorite drug.

"Rub it all over you," he heard himself say.

Jordan obeyed, bringing the shirt down his neck, rubbing it all over his pecs and erect little nipples, then his abs.

"The lower part of the shirt is dirty," Damiano said. "I came on it yesterday."

Jordan's hand froze, his pupils dilating. "You're disgusting," he said, unfolding the shirt and inspecting it. He found Damiano's dried spend very quickly. He stared at it with a strange, fixated expression. Before Damiano could say anything, Jordan brought the shirt back to his face and breathed in the soiled part of the fabric.

Jesus.

Damiano had never been harder in his life. Stroking his cock faster, he ordered, "Put it in your mouth."

"I hate you," Jordan moaned out, but he did put the soiled fabric into his mouth and suck on it, his other hand flying over his cock. "Oh god, this is so disgusting."

"You love it," Damiano said. "You're pathetic enough to suck on my dried come and be grateful for it."

Moaning, Jordan shoved two fingers wrapped in his soiled shirt deep into his mouth, his eyes closing in bliss as he came all over his hand and stomach.

The sight was enough to push Damiano over the edge, too.

He came, but he didn't feel satisfied.

The possessive beast in him wanted more.

***

The next time he made Jordan jerk off wearing only his shirt. It sated the hunger a little, but it wasn't enough. He knew this kind of possessiveness was ugly and creepy, but it still wasn't enough.

Damiano ended up fucking a fleshlight as he watched Jordan fuck his own mouth with his fingers. It was probably weird, but definitely not as weird as sending the fleshlight full of his come to Boston via express courier delivery.

"You're so gross," Jordan complained, as if Damiano couldn't see how hard his cock was. "Fuck, I can't believe I'm doing this," he moaned, fucking the fleshlight full of Damiano's jizz. "This is gross, and I hate you for making me do this."

It *was* gross. Damiano couldn't believe he was getting off on this, on watching another man fuck the dirty fleshlight he had used. But that was the appeal, in a fucked-up way. Possession. Ownership. He wanted his bodily fluids all over this man. To brand him in every possible way.

"Stop pretending you don't love it," Damiano said, unable to look away. "It turns you on, to put your cock where mine was, feel my dried jizz all over your cock."

Jordan moaned and came, filling the fleshlight with his come, their jizz mixing, and fuck, the thought nearly made him come too.

"Now rub the mess all over your body," Damiano said.

Jordan glared at the camera sulkily, as if Damiano couldn't see his cock twitch again.

But he did as he was told. He always did. It was nearly as heady as the orgasms, nearly as heady as the sight of Jordan rubbing their come all over his naked body and moaning, getting hard again. His muscular, shapely thighs were spread and Damiano's gaze was drawn to the tiny pink hole between them.

And the idea took root.

He had never really gotten the appeal of anal sex. He'd done anal a few times, but it had seemed like such a chore: why would he bother prepping a hole not intended for fucking when he could just stick his cock into a wet cunt? Jordan didn't have a cunt. But he had a hole that could be fucked. A hole he could put Damiano's come into. A hole to possess him through.

"Finger yourself," Damiano said harshly. "Put your dirty finger up your ass."

Jordan gave him an incredulous look. "No," he said mulishly. "That's going too far."

Ten minutes later, Damiano had him fingering his asshole.

He always got what he wanted. Or maybe Jordan was just very bad at saying no to him. He was still glaring at him, though.

"It feels weird," he grumbled, his brows furrowed in concentration. "Why do you even want me to do it? I'm not gay. *You* aren't gay."

"I want my come in you," Damiano said, watching him, transfixed. "You like it, too. Add another finger."

Jordan tried to add another, still frowning. "I need real lube. This hurts." Yet his cock was hard as a rock.

"You like it," Damiano said, his gaze traveling between Jordan's face and his spread thighs. "Does it feel good?"

"It feels weird," Jordan said again, but he was panting, his eyes unfocused and his face flushed. His rock-hard cock was nearly touching his abs. "But good weird. I'm not even sure I like it, but I don't want to pull my fingers out, either. I kind of get why gay men do it. There's this feeling of emptiness, like an itch I want to scratch."

Damiano hummed, stroking his cock harder.

"Fuck, I can hear you jacking off," Jordan said, moving his fingers faster. "It's not fair—I wanna see you too."

"Life isn't fair," Damiano said with a smile, his gaze fixed on Jordan's pink hole wrapped snugly around his two fingers.

"I hate you," Jordan said, panting, his eyes completely glazed over and his hips moving to meet his fingers. "At least send me a picture of your cock."

Damiano licked his lips, staring at Jordan's hole. "I can do better."

That was how he ended up sending Jordan a custom dildo shaped like his cock.

"It won't fit," Jordan said when he received it, as if Damiano couldn't see the way he was looking at it: with barely concealed hunger and fascination.

"You will make it fit," Damiano said, his voice turning hoarse at the sight of Jordan's fingers wrapped around the replica of his cock. "Suck it."

He stroked himself as he watched Jordan suck on the tip of his cock while he prepped his hole for it. "God, I can't believe what you turned me into," Jordan said breathlessly, licking the vein on the dildo as he put a fourth finger into his hole. "Can't believe I'm doing this."

"You've been gagging for my cock since the day we met," Damiano said. "You were just in denial."

"Arrogant dick," Jordan said, panting, his eyes glazed over. "Can I put it in now?"

"Yes, *caro*. Fuck yourself on my cock."

The sight of Jordan with his legs spread wide as he pushed the dildo into his hole was the most arousing thing he had ever seen. Damiano fucked into a fleshlight, imagining sinking into Jordan's body, the tightness and heat.

"Oh god," Jordan gasped out once the dildo was fully inside him.

"How does it feel?"

His eyes glassy and face flushed, Jordan moaned and moved the dildo in and out. "So good," he whispered. "Love it. Talk to me. Wanna hear your voice."

Damiano talked to him, fucking into the fleshlight and watching Jordan come apart on his cock. In other circumstances, he would have cringed at the filth he was spewing, the kind of filth that belonged in porn, saying some shit about chaining Jordan up to his bed and making him take his cock all the time until he couldn't live without it, until he was addicted to it and craved his cock when it wasn't in him.

Jordan came with a cry, his cock untouched, and panting like he'd run a marathon. "Fuck," he said, pulling the dildo out. "We're totally doing this again."

Damiano stared at Jordan's gaping, fucked-out hole. He wanted to lick it. He wanted to shove his tongue inside it. He wanted to slam his cock into it. He wanted to see his jizz leak out of it.

Fuck.

He had a problem.

# Chapter 21

The trouble with having bodyguards was that eventually people were bound to notice them.

Partly it was because his bodyguards had stopped trying to be very subtle now that Jordan knew about their presence. Partly it was because there were situations that made his bodyguards' presence very obvious. Like the celebration of his mother's birthday on a yacht his parents had hired just for that occasion.

"But why do you have bodyguards, dear?" his mother said, allowing Jordan to kiss her on a powdered cheek.

"Ferrara forced them on me," Jordan said, grimacing. "Work related stuff, nothing serious." He walked away quickly before his mother could question him further.

Fuck, he hated lying to his mother, but it wasn't like he could tell her the truth. He wasn't even sure what that truth was. *Mom, the bodyguards have been hired for me by an Italian mafia boss, who totally isn't my anything. Not a friend, not a lover, and definitely not a boyfriend. No one. I just jerk off with his penis-shaped dildo in my ass. Nothing to see here!*

Yeah, that would go well.

"Jord!"

He barely managed to turn at the sound of the familiar voice before his ex-wife crashed into him, hugging him hard with her slim arms.

Hesitantly, Jordan returned the hug.

"Hey, gorgeous," Bella said, pulling back and grinning.

She looked radiant and it took him a moment to realize what could be the reason: there was a noticeable bump in her belly.

Jordan's throat closed up. "You're pregnant?" he heard himself say.

Bella's grin faltered, becoming more hesitant. "Yes. Kurt and I are expecting a baby."

"Congratulations," he said, putting on his best smile. "I'm happy for you, Bel." He kissed her on the cheek and smiled wider. "Let's hope your kid will take after you and not Kurt. An innocent baby shouldn't be saddled with his looks."

She laughed. "You're awful! Kurt is good-looking! Not all of us have model-like looks like you!"

Jordan winked at her. "Don't let him hear you say that. You know how jealous he gets around me." He pretended to see someone behind her back. "I need to talk to someone, I have to go. See you around, Bel." He strode away, hoping he didn't look like he was fleeing.

Pushing through the crowd of guests, half of whom were already drunk, he grabbed a bottle of vodka and found a quiet spot on the lower deck.

He sat down in the darkest corner and stared at the water.

The sounds of laughter and cheerful conversations on the upper deck only made him feel more alone. Achingly lonely.

Opening the bottle, he brought it to his lips and took a big gulp. The vodka burned his throat, but it didn't quite erase the lump in it. He'd never felt more pathetic in his life.

He could be even more pathetic.

Pulling his phone out, Jordan found the right number—the number that he hadn't saved in his contacts—and pressed Call.

He didn't even know if the call would go through. He half-thought Damiano used a burner phone to call him, considering how paranoid he was. Even if it was Damiano's real phone, there was a high chance he wouldn't pick up anyway. He had never said Jordan could call him.

But Damiano answered. "One moment," he said before saying something in Italian. He clearly wasn't alone.

Jordan could hear him move, the sounds of doors closing, and then finally, "What's wrong? Why are you calling me?"

*I just wanted to hear your voice* sounded lame even in his head, so Jordan didn't say it.

But then again, Damiano had seen him at his worst and weakest. There was no use putting on the perfect Jordan Gates act around him.

"My ex-wife and her new husband are expecting a baby," Jordan said.

There was silence on the line.

Jordan could vividly imagine Damiano's dark brows furrowing as he tried to puzzle it out. God, he missed him so badly his stomach literally ached with it.

"And that upsets you why?" Damiano said, his voice terse. "Are you jealous?"

Jordan took another swig from the bottle, and then another. "No—yes."

He sighed. "I don't know." He stared at the city's lights in the distance. "We found out that I couldn't have kids three years ago. Our marriage fell apart soon after that." He chuckled. "You know, it's funny. I didn't even think I wanted to have kids all that much until I was told I couldn't have them and I was shooting blanks. It's just… It made me feel like less of a man, you know?"

"That's stupid," Damiano said derisively. "Procreation is hardly a man's only function. If your ex-wife couldn't understand it—"

"No, Bel was amazing," Jordan said. "Very understanding. She started looking at *options*, but…" He took another swig from the bottle and set it down, feeling a little dizzy already, his tongue not quite listening to him. It'd been a while since he consumed alcohol.

"I couldn't stand it," Jordan mumbled, his stomach roiling with the old self-loathing. Or maybe it was the vodka. "I didn't like the idea of raising another man's kid, having it around constantly as a reminder of me not being a real man."

His lips twisted into something ugly. "Remember you told me about Marco keeping you around because he loved your mother? Apparently I couldn't do the same. The whole thing made me realize that I no longer loved Bel, that I couldn't love another man's child—that the baby being a piece of her wasn't enough for me. So we got a divorce. And now she has a real man who gave her the baby she wanted so much, and I'm—well, you know what I am."

He smiled bitterly, his vision swimming. "A total wreck whining to you about my woes because hearing your voice makes me feel better."

There was silence on the line again.

But Jordan could feel that Damiano was still there.

Could feel him, across the four thousand miles that separated them.

"You know the funniest part?" Jordan mumbled. He was slurring. Fuck, he'd drunk too much. He should probably shut up before he said something he might regret. But he didn't seem to be able to stop. He wanted to say it. "I would totally raise *your* kids." He laughed. "I love your dirty shirts, your sweat, and your jizz. Of course I'd love it if you gave me your baby. So if you have any babies lying around, you can send them to me—they'll be the most spoiled babies in the world."

He heard Damiano inhale unsteadily and then exhale. "Stop talking, Jordan," he said, his voice sounding strange. "You're drunk. Go to bed."

Jordan pouted. "You're no fun. Don't want to go to bed here. I didn't bring my dildo with me—can't sleep without your cock in me."

Damiano swore in Italian and hung up.

Rude.

Scowling, Jordan glared at his phone, staring at the picture of Damiano on his screen. He kissed it, feeling beyond pathetic but too drunk to care.

Hopefully he would forget all of this tomorrow.

# Chapter 22

Damiano left his private jet, gave his passport to Lorenzo to get him through passport control, and headed toward the waiting car, ignoring the gloomy look on Lorenzo's normally blank face. He had no patience for his complaints now.

Lorenzo had already expressed his displeasure at Damiano's decision to travel to New York City personally to oversee the handling of some upstarts from the American mafia there who had encroached on their territory. Lorenzo hated transatlantic flights and hated wasting time. "Paolo could have handled the Gambino family," he kept grumbling. "Their little stunt isn't worth our time, boss."

Truth be told, he turned out to be correct.

Damiano ended up watching dispassionately as the Gambino patriarch was taught a lesson. His heir was very eager to please afterward and gave him a lot of concessions as they struck a new deal. The whole ordeal was over in less than four hours, with minimal life losses on both sides.

"Back to Italy, boss?" Lorenzo said as they got into a car and headed back to the airport. "Or to Boston?"

Damiano pinned him with a cold look and took some pleasure in making his right-hand man squirm in discomfort. "And why would I go to Boston?" he said, his voice carefully emotionless.

Lorenzo's Adam's apple bobbed.

Damiano waited, his gaze on the other man.

Lorenzo fidgeted. "I just thought you might want to check on the—on the mark there, since you're in the country and all."

Damiano looked out the window at the New York scenery. It pissed him off how transparent he apparently was.

It had been two months since he'd last seen him in person.

*Just a quick check. Who would it hurt? You're in the country anyway.*

Damiano gritted his teeth, irritated with himself. It was pretty telling how used he was to this bullshit that these kinds of thoughts didn't even surprise him anymore. They had occurred regularly for the past half a year with aggravating persistence.

"If it's all the same to you, I'd like to go straight home," Lorenzo said. "I still have to buy presents for the kids."

Right. Christmas was just two days away.

His mood darkening, Damiano stared blankly at the Christmas-decorated stores they were driving past. It wasn't exactly his favorite time of the year, which was why he'd taken the excuse to leave Italy. He couldn't escape from Christmas in America, but at least he didn't have the family here, people who couldn't stand him and tolerated him on Christmas because they were scared shitless of what he'd do if they didn't. He knew he probably had a gazillion Christmas presents from every member of the family waiting for him back home, every present carefully picked to please him. He had no intention of opening a single one.

"Tell the pilot we're going to Boston," Damiano said curtly. And before Lorenzo could get *ideas*, he added, "To visit my stepbrother."

"Right away, boss," Lorenzo said after a moment and pulled his phone out.

Damiano didn't listen to his conversation with the pilot. He stared out the window at the festively decorated streets and wondered who was going to be more unhappy with his visit: he or Raffaele.

It started snowing.

***

It was snowing in Boston, too.

Damiano accepted a dark winter coat from the flight attendant and shrugged into it before leaving the jet.

Lorenzo left to buy presents for his kids while Damiano got into a different car and headed to Raffaele's house by himself. Well, himself and four vans of bodyguards, but they didn't count. He barely noticed them. Though Raffaele was undoubtedly going to notice them.

The thought made Damiano smile faintly. Pissing off Raffaele and ruining his Christmas with his visit was going to be at least somewhat entertaining. It should hopefully distract him sufficiently and prevent him from any inadvisable decisions.

The two-story house was fairly small by Ferrara family standards, but nauseatingly picturesque, illuminated by Christmas lights.

Damiano got out of the car and stared at it, wondering once again what he was doing here.

But if he were to save face and prove Lorenzo wrong, he had to follow through. He wasn't here for Jordan.

He wasn't, damn it.

Sighing, Damiano walked to the door and pressed the buzzer.

Raffaele was as pissed as Damiano expected.

"What the hell are you doing here?" he ground out, glaring at his security detail.

"Merry Christmas to you too, brother," Damiano said, pushing into the house past him.

The house looked even more nauseatingly homely and picturesque on the inside than it did on the outside. Damiano had trouble believing that the cheerful decor was Raffaele's idea.

He was proven correct when he noticed a blond guy standing on a stool, decorating the Christmas tree. "Who is that?" the guy said, before turning around. "Oh."

For a moment, Damiano's breath caught in his throat. The guy looked a lot like…

But of course he did. The resemblance was the sole reason Raffaele had paid another man to play the role of his boyfriend for the duration of his visit, after all.

"I'm Nate," the guy said, jumping off the stool and walking over to shake his hand. "Are you Raffaele's relative? You look like you're Italian." He gave an embarrassed laugh. "Not that all Italians look like each other, but…" His laugh petered out when he glanced at Raffaele. "Um, right. So this is awkward."

From up close, there were more differences than similarities: Nate's blue eyes were more open, less guarded, his expression kind. Not that Jordan wasn't kind—he was, but he didn't wear his heart on his sleeve like this guy did.

"This is Damiano," Raffaele ground out from behind him. "And he's already leaving."

Nate rolled his eyes.

"Don't be an asshole," he hissed at his boyfriend before smiling sheepishly at Damiano. "So you're Raffaele's brother!"

"Stepbrother," Damiano said, taking off his coat.

"Barely," Raffaele grunted, earning a kick from his boyfriend before Nate turned to him with an apologetic smile.

"Please make yourself at home, and I'm really sorry for this one," Nate said, gesturing to Raffaele.

Damiano dropped his coat on the chair. "Don't worry. We grew up together, so I'm used to it."

Raffaele crossed his arms over his chest and glared at him. "What are you doing here?" he said again.

Damiano smiled, taking a seat in the comfortable armchair by the fireplace. "Isn't it appropriate to visit family this time of the year? Where's your Christmas spirit?"

The look Raffaele gave him was decidedly unimpressed. "You have one minute to explain yourself or I'm kicking you out of the house, and I don't care how many goons you brought with you."

"What goons?" Nate said, walking to the window. He whistled. "How are we going to explain that to the neighbors?" He chuckled. "Damn, I feel like Aunt Petunia fretting over appearing normal and respectable."

When Raffaele and Damiano gave him blank looks, Nate shook his head, his expression incredulous.

"Seriously? Never mind. All right, I'll go see if we have some beer while you two… talk."

He left, presumably for the kitchen, leaving them in thick, strained silence.

Damiano pulled out a cigarette and lit it.

Raffaele bored his black eyes into him, his expression

somewhere between frustrated and furious.

"I swear to god, Damiano," he said, switching to Italian. "Explain yourself. What the fuck are you doing here? I didn't distance myself from the family for nothing. I don't want to be connected to the family business. You turning up here with a gaggle of forty bodyguards isn't conducive to that."

Taking a long drag from his cigarette, Damiano said, "I'm in the States on business, so I can't exactly go around without security. Sorry if I'm inconveniencing your perfect, tidy American life, but you'll have to suck it up. I'm staying here for Christmas." He switched to English and said with a smile, "We both know you won't kick me out and risk upsetting the mentally unstable sociopath around your precious boyfriend."

Stiffening, Raffaele peered at him cautiously. "Who told you that I called you that?"

Damiano shrugged, taking another drag. "There's very little that doesn't reach my ears, brother dearest."

A sigh.

"Why are you really here, Damiano?" Raffaele said, pinching the bridge of his nose.

Damiano gave him a flat look. Did he really think he was going to explain himself?

Raffaele studied him for a long moment. "Are you here to see Jordan?"

It took every bit of his self-control to keep his expression blank. "Jordan?" he said, feigning faint bewilderment. "Who is that?"

Raffaele eyed him for a while. He was an exceptionally smart, observant man. But he had always lost to him when they had played poker: he wasn't good at reading him.

Damiano could tell that he bought it—bought that Jordan had been so insignificant in the grand scheme of things that Damiano might have actually forgotten his name half a year later.

The fact that Raffaele believed it made it all the more aggravating that it wasn't true. Jordan *should* have been insignificant enough for him to forget him. This… obsession was so wildly out of character for him that of course Raffaele had believed his lie.

His mood changing for the worse, Damiano got to his feet. "Show me my room," he said curtly, walking deeper into the house.

Behind him, Raffaele sighed, but as Damiano had expected, he acquiesced. Of course he did. He wouldn't risk upsetting the unstable sociopath around his boyfriend. People with significant others were so predictable it was mind-numbingly boring to manipulate them.

He had thought Raffaele would be more of a challenge—he used to be—but it seemed caring for someone made him weak.

It always did.

***

Dinner was a quiet affair. Nate did most of the talking, and somehow managed not to sound awkward at all while doing it. He was one of those friendly, easy-going guys that were instantly likable.

Damiano still found it hard to like him. He looked too much like Jordan and somehow *not enough* like Jordan. He was irritated with himself for being unable to stop making those comparisons—and for thinking about the fact that the real thing was just a few miles away.

No. He wasn't here for this, damn it. It was one thing to keep calling Jordan and watching him jerk off like a creep, and completely another to enable his obsession and actually visit him in person.

He wouldn't do it.

He wouldn't.

*You know the funniest part? I would totally raise* your *kids.*

Damiano stabbed the piece of beef on his plate with his fork, put it into his mouth, and chewed aggressively.

Try as he might, he couldn't forget that drunken confession. The words were innocuous, but what they implied wasn't—and he kept fixating on it, unable to forget.

Unable to let go.

# Chapter 23

Jordan set down the last present and surveyed his handiwork. Every present for his family was accounted for, every single one of them meticulously chosen and perfectly wrapped. A Christmas tree was twinkling merrily in the corner by the living room window, perfectly decorated. He'd even hung Christmas stockings over his fake fireplace. Everything looked perfect.

He still couldn't feel the Christmas spirit, his mood gloomy and his heart not really in it.

He knew why, of course. He tried not to think about it, but he couldn't lie to himself. He felt down because Christmas was about spending time with loved ones, and the person he wanted to see the most wouldn't be around. It made him feel cold on the inside.

Sighing, Jordan got to his feet and went to the bathroom. Maybe a hot shower would help him feel warmer.

His soapy hands trailed over his body, teasing over his nipples, which immediately hardened, and then stroking his stomach before wrapping around his half-hard cock. He gave it a few uninterested strokes before ignoring it in favor of his hole. He was so used to having something inside him these days that he easily slipped two fingers in.

He gasped and set his feet wider, enjoying the slight burn and stretch. He almost didn't like using lube—it didn't burn as much with lube. He liked it a little rough, Jordan had found.

But soon, the fingers weren't enough. Jordan pulled them out before turning the water off and reaching for the lube on the shelf. He generously lubed up the suction-cupped dildo on the wall, stroking the familiar girth and shape with relish. The first dildo Damiano had sent him didn't have a suction cup function. It was in his bedside drawer and got very regular use. This one Jordan had ordered himself, an exact replica of the other one but with a suction-cup base. He used it when he got horny in the shower and wanted Damiano's cock in him pronto.

Jordan turned his back to the dildo, lined it up with his hole, and slowly pushed back onto it, groaning at the stretch. So fucking good. He couldn't believe he'd spent thirty-two years of his life having no idea how good having a cock in his asshole felt. It made him feel like a total cock slut, but these days Jordan couldn't go without being fucked in the ass once a day at the very least. He knew he was completely addicted to this feeling, but he didn't know how to stop. It was the only thing that made him feel good outside of Damiano's calls: the replica of Damiano's cock filling him up and making him feel complete.

Panting hard, Jordan moved his hips, fucking himself on the thick cock and imagining that it was Damiano standing behind him, fucking him hard—

The doorbell rang.

Jordan froze, his eyes flying open. Maybe he could ignore whoever it was and they would go away.

Gritting his teeth, he resumed moving, fucking himself on the cock.

The doorbell rang again.

Swearing under his breath, Jordan pulled off of the dildo with great reluctance and pulled a white robe over his bare shoulders, tying it loosely around his waist. More than a little irritated, Jordan strode toward the door. He was so hard he was close to crying from frustration, his hole clenching around nothing, greedy for cock.

He yanked the door open, but his scathing remark died on his lips when he saw the tall man in a dark coat standing on the other side.

For a moment, Jordan was sure it wasn't real. It must have been a dream. How many dreams like this had he had? Too many to count.

But it felt so real.

Damiano stared at him, his gaze dark and unreadable. He looked mouthwateringly good, as usual. Even more so than usual, because the melting snow on his dark eyelashes and hair added a brightness to him that made him look unbearably attractive.

Jordan swallowed. He felt too hot, still too desperate and aroused to think clearly, his cock throbbing under his robe and he was this close to—this close to jumping Damiano and climbing him like a monkey. Which was ridiculous, because he was a lot bigger than a monkey, but it was what he burned to do. Climb this man and cling to him. And then pull out his cock and ride it hard. Not necessarily in that order.

"You're home," Damiano said. There was a faint accusation in his voice, as if he didn't expect him to be at home.

"Where else would I be at ten in the evening?" Jordan croaked out, gripping the door frame. "And don't you have cameras in my apartment?"

"I thought you might be with your family," Damiano said, still looking at him accusingly even as he reached out and grabbed a fistful of Jordan's robe, dragging him close. "And no, I left my laptop in Italy."

Their foreheads pressed together, and Jordan had no thoughts left, his mind going utterly blank. He inhaled Damiano's scent greedily, his body trembling with violent need. He sank his shaking fingers into Damiano's hair, reveling in the familiar texture. Damiano's breathing hitched, but he didn't move.

God, he couldn't fucking stand it. He wanted to *consume* him. He wanted to suck on his tongue until he passed out from lack of air.

With a defeated groan, Jordan crushed their mouths together—and everything else disappeared.

Damiano made an inhuman sound and kissed back, as forcefully, shoving his tongue down Jordan's throat. They both moaned in relief—and hunger. So much hunger. Jordan couldn't kiss him as deeply as he wanted to. He whined in frustration, sucking on Damiano's tongue like it was the holy grail, his hands roaming all over the other man's firm body, dragging his coat off. It fell to the ground and Jordan fumbled with Damiano's belt and fly, pulling Damiano inside his apartment.

Finally, he had Damiano's cock in his hand, hot, hard, and perfect. The shape of it was so familiar, but his dildos had nothing on the real thing's texture and warmth. Desperate, Jordan untied his robe and let it fall to the floor. "Fuck me," he breathed against Damiano's mouth, stroking his cock greedily. "Fuck me, or I'll fucking explode and die."

Damiano laughed hoarsely as Jordan attempted to climb his body and sit on his cock.

"Easy," he ground out. "I can't fuck you like this. You need prep."

"I'm ready," Jordan said, kissing all over Damiano's jaw and muscular neck, whatever he could reach, cradling his face greedily. "I was fucking myself on my dildo when you rang the doorbell. Give me the real thing."

Damiano cursed and shoved him face first to the wall. Jordan knocked his nose against the wall, and it hurt like a bitch, but he didn't care: he arched his back like a slut as firm fingers gripped his hips. Distantly, he was aware that they were barely inside his apartment, and the door was still open, and anyone could come across them, but he didn't give a fuck. He'd been craving this for half a year. He didn't care if all of the building was watching them.

"Come on," he gasped, his mind blank but for the molten need. "Need your cock in me."

Biting him at the back of his neck, Damiano *slammed* into him in one long thrust.

Jordan cried out, his eyes rolling to the back of his head. Oh god, oh god, oh god. Such fullness and heat. So good. His dildos had nothing on the real thing, on the real man.

Damiano started fucking him, hard and fast, his fingers holding Jordan's hips in an iron grip, his face buried in Jordan's nape. It burned a little but every time Damiano pulled out, Jordan found himself craving more. His hips were moving, chasing the pain-pleasure, his voice sounding absolutely wrecked as he moaned. He was too loud, he knew that, but he couldn't seem to contain himself.

Damiano fucked like a machine, perfectly in control of his movements but with so much power. Soon enough, he set a punishing pace that rendered Jordan helpless, only capable of gripping the door frame and taking it.

He wanted to come so badly, but he never wanted this to end, either, so he tried to stave off his orgasm, but he couldn't—he couldn't—

His orgasm was ripped out of him, the most intense one in his life, and Jordan sobbed out, his hole clenching hard around the cock in him. The man behind him grunted, his breathing growing harsher. He thrust a few more times and went rigid, spilling into him. Panting, Damiano sagged against him, heavy and perfect. God.

God.

Jordan found himself smiling dazedly. It was perfect. Everything was perfect. He never wanted this moment to end. Never wanted them to be separated again.

The sound of approaching footsteps startled Jordan from his blissed-out state.

Shit. They were barely inside his apartment. The door was open. He was fully naked, with another man's cock in him, even if Damiano was still mostly dressed.

Frantically, Jordan pushed Damiano off, barely managed to grab Damiano's coat from the floor and all but jumped into the apartment. He caught a glimpse of Mrs. Brown, an elderly woman from the fourth floor, before the door slammed shut.

Jordan fell on his ass and burst out laughing.

"I'm glad one of us finds it amusing," Damiano said, very dryly.

Still chuckling, Jordan looked up. Oh.

It was positively unfair how flawless this man could look after fucking his brains out. Damiano had already fixed his fly and there was nothing betraying what he'd been doing a few minutes ago. He could have stepped off a GQ cover, with his thick, glossy dark hair, piercing eyes, and the perfect, angular symmetry of his face.

Jordan sighed and covered his eyes with his hands. Maybe if he didn't see that face, he'd get a few brain cells back. He needed them, in order not to behave like a clingy, desperate cock slut. He still had some self-respect left. Not a lot, considering the fact that he'd all but begged Damiano to fuck him the moment he saw him.

"What are you doing in Boston?" Jordan said into his hands.

Silence.

"I came to visit Raffaele," Damiano said stiffly.

Taking his hands away, Jordan gave him an incredulous look. "Try again," he said, not bothering to hide his amusement.

Damiano glowered at him, his jawline tense in a way it got only when he was truly pissed off. Fuck, he was so hot when he was angry.

Jordan sighed on the inside, exasperated with himself. He got to his feet, becoming very much aware of his nudity when Damiano's eyes raked over him hungrily. Talk about mixed signals.

"You must have missed him terribly," Jordan said, stepping to Damiano and pressing his naked body to his fully clothed one.

"What?" Damiano said after a moment, so obviously distracted it would have been hilarious if Jordan hadn't felt as distracted by his proximity.

God, it was ridiculous. He'd just had the best orgasm of his life, but he already felt hungry for more, his skin crawling with the need for closeness. With need for this man. The need wasn't even sexual, not truly, but it was the only way it could manifest, the only way it could be sated.

"Raffaele," Jordan whispered, leaning their foreheads together.

"You said you came to visit him. Did you miss him?"

Damiano kissed the corner of his mouth. "Yes," he said dazedly, his hands gripping Jordan's ass and pulling him flush against him.

"Did you think of him all the time?" Jordan whispered, rubbing their mouths together, the touch barely there but causing his lips to tremble.

"Yes," Damiano said, biting his bottom lip. "All the time."

Jordan parted his lips. "He thought of you all the time, too. Kiss me."

Damiano did.

And nothing else mattered for a long time.

Only him.

# Chapter 24

Jordan had never really thought he had a high libido. His sex drive had always been good, nothing crazy. He wasn't really the type of man to think of sex non-stop. He wasn't the type to laze in bed with a lover for a day.

Until he suddenly was.

He and Damiano had had sex on every surface of his apartment over the past forty hours: the couch, the floor, the table in the kitchen, and of course, the bed—three times. It should have been physically impossible to have so much sex for a man in his thirties. But apparently his body hadn't gotten the memo that he wasn't a randy teenager anymore—it wanted more, no matter how much sex they had already had.

"Oh my god, get out," Jordan groaned as he found himself reaching for more kisses again. He buried his face in his pillow and groaned again.

Damiano, the asshole, laughed and kissed him on the nape, which definitely wasn't helping.

Jordan blindly grabbed his hand and entwined their fingers together. Yep, apparently not only did he have a bad case of teenage horniness, he was also acting like a teenager, too. A very sappy one.

Sighing, Damiano allowed it, the position forcing him to wrap his arm over Jordan's back. Or maybe they were just cuddling. That hardly would be anything unusual for them. Though normally Jordan was on his back when they did it.

"I need to go," Damiano said, sinking his teeth into Jordan's shoulder.

"You said that a few hours ago already." At least he wasn't the only pathetic one.

"I needed to go hours ago," Damiano said, his tone grim. "I needed to go yesterday."

Jordan's stomach tightened into a hard, uncomfortable knot. "Yeah. I'm supposed to be at my parents' house this evening. They have something of a Christmas party on Christmas Eve every year. It's a tradition. Frankly, I would already be there by now. They're probably expecting me already."

A few seconds passed.

"You should go," Jordan said.

Neither of them moved.

"One last time," Damiano said, pushing Jordan's leg up and slipping back into him.

"Are you kidding me?" Jordan said with a half groan, half laugh, but his mind was already clouding, his loose hole accepting Damiano's cock easily. He was so wet that his hole made obscene, sloppy sounds on every thrust. He already had so much come in him that Jordan was pretty sure he could see it: his normally flat stomach was a little round. Full of Damiano's jizz. To his embarrassment, the sight actually turned him on. There was a weird sort of appeal to it.

Damiano fucked him slowly, fingers gripping his hips. Jordan squirmed, partly in discomfort, partly in pleasure. He might have had a dildo in him on a regular basis, but he had never had a gay sex marathon like this. He was sore. The cock was moving inside him relentlessly, and Jordan whimpered, oversensitive and overwhelmed. Part of him wanted this to stop, his thighs straining, arms cramping, body melting in sweat. The bed was creaking, and he felt like a helpless ragdoll under the force of Damiano's thrusts. It was almost too much.

But it felt too good. He felt like a junkie in need of another fix, even though he knew the drug was bad for him. He didn't care how sore he was. He wanted as much as Damiano was willing to give, and he would spread his legs as long as Damiano wanted to fuck him.

He was so focused on Damiano that he barely noticed his own orgasm, his noises breaking into weak, ragged gasps and moans as he came. "Oh god! God…"

The long, heavy pumping into his ass changed to hard, rough grinding, more like animal rutting than thrusting. Jordan grabbed his own cheeks and spread them, eager. *Please, please, please. Come in me.* He craved it desperately, he needed to feel Damiano's come in him, to declare in the brutal honesty of bodies and bodily fluids that Damiano wanted him. He wanted Damiano's orgasm more than he had wanted his own.

Muttering something in Italian in a low, hoarse voice, Damiano slammed hard into him, and Jordan felt him come. After so many times over the past two days, Jordan was so familiar with the hot rush of come pouring into him—thick, potent gushes, chest heaving against his back as Damiano ground each wad nice and deep, and Jordan let out a long, wanton moan, feeling like a slut. He was a slut, a slut for this man. How could having another man's cock in his asshole feel so good?

The pleasure wasn't even fully physical. It was all in his head. He liked feeling Damiano's softened cock in him, proof of his desire. Proof that he wanted Jordan, that he couldn't get enough of him, even after so many orgasms.

Jordan opened his eyes and looked at his stomach. Was it his imagination or did it look more bloated now? He stared at it in morbid fascination.

His phone on the nightstand went off and Jordan shifted his gaze to it. He considered not picking up. But it was probably his sister or his mother wondering where he was. If he didn't answer, he wouldn't put it past them to come here and check on him.

With great reluctance, Jordan reached for his phone. It was his sister, as he had expected.

"Where the hell are you?" Eloise said the moment he answered. "Why haven't you been answering our messages?"

Messages?

"I was asleep," Jordan said.

"It's two in the afternoon," Eloise said, her voice full of skepticism.

They both knew he wasn't one to laze in bed even during weekends.

"What did you want, Eloise?" Jordan said, avoiding answering the unasked question.

"Mom is panicking because Mrs. Hudson knocked over the wine bottles, and now we have no wine for dinner! Dad will have a stroke if we serve some cheap wine from Whole Foods."

"Pretty sure there's some expensive stuff there too," Jordan said distractedly. He was distracted by the strong fingers grazing lightly against his hip, the contrast between Damiano's gorgeous darker skin and his own pale skin fascinating.

"You know what a wine snob Dad is," Eloise said. "So drag your ass out of bed and go get some good wine before he finds out what Mrs. Hudson did."

"You know I understand nothing about wine!" Jordan said, but Eloise had already hung up.

Great.

"Who is Mrs. Hudson?" Damiano said into his ear.

Shivering, Jordan turned his head and pressed his cheek against Damiano's. Neither of them had shaved since Damiano's arrival, but unlike his own barely noticeable stubble, Damiano's was closer to scruff. It felt delicious against his skin. "Mmm?"

"Mrs. Hudson," Damiano said, kissing along his jawline. "The one who knocked over the wine."

"Oh. She's…" Jordan gasped, turning his head and seeking Damiano's mouth. He wanted kisses. It was frankly alarming how thirsty for this man he still was despite the non-stop sex marathon "A cat. She's a cat. Kiss me. One last time. And then I'll have to go."

Damiano kissed him.

It wasn't the last one.

About an hour later, Jordan finally managed to get out of bed—and only because his phone wouldn't stop ringing. Eloise could be annoyingly persistent.

"Holy shit," he swore, grabbing the wall as dull pain shot through his lower body. He'd never gotten this sore from dildos. This was something else. Turning his head, he glared at Damiano but quickly turned away because the bastard looked so kissable lounging naked in bed, his hair tousled and his eyes soft with satisfaction. Ugh.

"Fuck, I don't think I can drive like this, much less search for some 'good wine' by my dad's standards."

"I can give you a lift," Damiano said.

Jordan bit his bottom lip, hesitating. He knew he should say no. It was a terrible idea. It was very clear that he couldn't be trusted to be alone with this man, given how reluctant to part from him he still felt after nearly two days of non-stop sex and who knew how many orgasms. He should say no and hail a cab.

But.

"Do you know anything about wine?"

***

Lorenzo looked less than impressed when he saw Jordan walking—half-limping—to the car. But his pinched expression quickly shifted into one of blankness when Damiano shot him a cold look.

Damiano said something in Italian, Lorenzo nodded and got into the driver's seat, and then they were off.

Jordan reclined in the backseat, trying to take the pressure off his sore ass. Maybe they should stop by a drugstore and he could buy something for it. But fuck, how would he even ask for something like that?

He was still mulling it over when the car came to a stop. "Are we there already?" Jordan said, looking out the window. He'd rather not look at Damiano unless he had to. He didn't trust himself.

"No," Damiano said as Lorenzo got out of the car. "We stopped at a pharmacy. Lorenzo will buy something for your soreness."

Jordan stared at him. "Lorenzo will buy something for my soreness?" he choked out. "Why would he do it?"

Damiano looked infuriatingly unflappable—and still infuriatingly attractive. "I told him," he said simply.

"You told him. That my asshole is sore."

A corner of Damiano's mouth twitched. "Yes."

"I can't fucking believe you," Jordan said, groaning and covering his face with his hands. "I hate you. How am I supposed to look him in the eye?"

Damiano, the dick, laughed. "Easily. Ignore him. It's his job to do as he's told. Nothing more, nothing less."

"It's easy for you to say when you aren't the one walking bowlegged."

"That's precisely why I sent Lorenzo to the drugstore. You can't go to your family dinner like this."

Jordan couldn't argue with that logic.

"You should have told me you were that sore. I didn't want to hurt you."

Jordan removed his hands and looked at him. Damiano's expression was a little uncomfortable and he held himself stiffly, but his eyes shone with sincerity.

Jordan hoped he didn't look as lovesick as he felt. Darting forward, he buried his hand in Damiano's hair and kissed him softly. Or at least it was supposed be a soft, short kiss. But his lips parted for Damiano's tongue, and the kiss quickly turned needy. God, he was beginning to get scared that he'd never get enough of this man.

An awkward cough made them finally part.

Jordan tore his gaze away from Damiano's lips and half-lidded eyes and stared blankly at Lorenzo, who looked like he'd swallowed a lemon as he handed him a package before turning away and starting the car.

Right.

His face burning, Jordan looked at the ointment Lorenzo had bought and wondered if it was possible to expire from sheer mortification.

***

It turned out that Damiano did know a thing or two about wine. Almost too much, in fact. He was as much of a wine snob as Jordan's father was, sneering at the expensive wine Jordan personally considered quite good—but apparently he was very wrong.

Rolling his eyes, Jordan was left trailing after Damiano and the wine store owner as the elderly man showed off his rare wine collection to Damiano.

There were no other customers—Jordan suspected that the store catered to high-profile clients and was opened on a holiday at Damiano's request. There were certainly no price tags in an establishment like that, and Jordan didn't bother asking how much the wine Damiano ended up picking cost. He saw no point in making a fuss about something that was a drop in the ocean for Damiano.

There was also a horrible, shameful part of him that liked it: liked that Damiano was wasting his valuable time on choosing wine for Jordan's family.

The direction of his own thoughts annoyed and embarrassed him, but there was nothing Jordan could do about it. Nor could he do anything about the ridiculously inappropriate, possessive feeling that stirred in his stomach every time he looked at Damiano. *This is my man*, it whispered with vicious satisfaction. *Look how knowledgeable, powerful, and attractive he is.*

It was deeply mortifying.

Damiano wasn't his anything, much less *his man*, what the fuck.

He was his own man, and he didn't need another powerful man to feel good about himself.

At least the ointment Lorenzo had bought seemed to be working.

Jordan had applied it in the wine store's bathroom while Damiano talked to the owner. It worked like a charm. He still felt a little sore and sensitive, but he could walk normally now, which was a relief, because Jordan hadn't been looking forward to trying to explain to his family why he was walking funny.

He wasn't looking forward to dinner at all, to be honest. Normally he loved Christmas dinners at his parents' house with his extended family in attendance, but right now… His stomach knotted up at the mere thought of saying goodbye to Damiano and not seeing him for who knew how long. They hadn't really talked about what they had been doing—what the sex meant, if it even meant anything.

Would Damiano disappear from his life again? Or would he stick to the phone sex they had been having? Or maybe the sex had cured Damiano of this weird thing, and this was it. Jordan didn't feel cured in the least—if anything, he felt like he'd gotten reinfected with the disease, feeling clingy as hell—but that was him. Maybe Damiano felt differently.

"What's up with that face?" Damiano said as they got into the car.

Jordan sighed, grimacing and glaring at his own hands. He could see Damiano's hand in his peripheral vision and it was taking everything in him not to grab it. Fuck, he really was turning into a teenage girl. He'd never been one to hold hands, only tolerating it when his girlfriends and wife had initiated it.

"I hate how clingy I feel," he said, pulling a face. "This isn't me."

Damiano hummed and looked out the window. Jordan could no longer see his face, only the tight line of his sharp jawline.

Then, his fingers moved, inching closer to Jordan's, until they touched the back of his hand.

His heart somewhere in his throat, Jordan stared at them before turning his hand and entangling their fingers.

Christ, how could something so simple feel so intense?

"Come with me to the party," he blurted out before he could stop himself.

Silence.

"As a friend," Jordan added, clearing his throat.

After a long moment, Damiano gave a clipped nod.

# Chapter 25

There was a surreal quality to the whole evening.

Jordan had never imagined Damiano being in the same room as his family. They represented different parts of his life, and seeing Damiano converse with his parents was bizarre.

It didn't feel wrong, though. There was something satisfying about having Damiano in his childhood home, surrounded by his family, and it kept feeding the possessiveness Jordan was trying to quash.

"Jesus, take a picture," Eloise said, nearly making Jordan jump. "If you keep staring at him that way, you'll catch fire. There are kids around, Jord."

"Don't know what you mean," Jordan said.

His sister rolled her eyes and wrapped her arm around his waist. "He's very handsome," she said. "But I had no idea you swung this way."

"I don't," Jordan said, honestly enough. He still didn't consider himself bi. Damiano was the only man he'd ever found attractive on a personal level.

She smirked, giving Damiano a once-over. "Right. But this man can certainly make even the straightest guy slightly bent. Yummy. Just looking at him makes me a little wet."

"Don't be gross. You're married."

"I'm married, not dead," she said. "I can appreciate a fine man when I see one. Paul isn't the possessive type." She snorted, glancing at him. "Though it looks like you are."

"I'm not possessive," Jordan said.

"Please," Eloise said. "You look like you're one step away from strangling me for daring to look at your man this way."

"He isn't my anything," Jordan said, his stomach clenching at the truth of those words. Damiano wasn't his anything. He had no real claim to him.

His sister's gaze turned serious as she studied him. "But do you want him to be your something?"

Jordan didn't reply. Thankfully Eloise's youngest took that moment to throw an apple at his brother, which promptly made Eddie burst out crying, and Eloise hurried off, her interrogation forgotten.

But Jordan couldn't forget her words. *Do you want him to be your something?*

Her words were still on his mind during dinner. Damiano wasn't seated next to him—Jordan's mother was too particular about her seating arrangements to allow an unexpected guest to mess with them—and Jordan ended up watching Damiano from the other end of the table and thinking about his sister's words.

He knew what the answer to her question was, of course: *yes. Fuck yes.* He would let Damiano put a fucking collar on him with his name on it, anything to have tangible proof of meaning something to him. Something significant. Something that would make their relationship real. Because he often felt like his life consisted of nothing but waiting for Damiano's call and being stressed if he didn't hear from him for a few days.

He hated it.

Hated the utter lack of control over their relationship, hated that if something happened to Damiano, no one would even notify Jordan, because he was a dirty little secret, a weakness Damiano was ashamed of. Damiano had even come to Boston under the pretense of visiting his estranged stepbrother, not Jordan. There was nothing tying them together. Nothing but their messy feelings. Nothing permanent.

Jordan frowned, looking at his hands.

At the ring on his finger.

***

They left Jordan's parents' house well after midnight.

It was snowing again, large snowflakes falling onto Damiano's dark hair as they walked slowly toward the parked cars.

"Thanks," Jordan said quietly, lifting his face and closing his eyes as snowflakes fell onto his overheated cheeks. "For putting up with my father all evening. He can get carried away when he discusses politics and wine."

Damiano just hummed. He didn't lie that it was no bother to him. Jordan knew he was introverted and big social gatherings weren't really his thing.

"At least his conversation was reasonably intelligent," Damiano said, coming to a halt and looking at him. It was hard to read his expression in the light of the street lamps. "Your bodyguards will take you home in their car. I can't be seen much by your apartment complex. It's not safe."

Right.

"Will I see you before you go home?" He was impressed with how casual his voice sounded.

Damiano shook his head, the line of his shoulders tense. "My plane is leaving within the hour."

Oh.

It must have been nice to have a private jet that let you leave the country—and unwanted feelings—whenever you wanted to.

The package in Jordan's pocket seemed to burn him through his coat.

*Just give it to him.*

Looking at the snow at his feet, Jordan said, "I have something for you." Slipping his hand into his pocket, he retrieved the package and handed it to Damiano.

"A Christmas gift?"

Jordan's lips twisted. "Sort of." He didn't look as Damiano opened it.

"It's a ring." Damiano had never sounded so *baffled*. It almost made Jordan smile. Almost. He didn't really feel like smiling. His throat felt uncomfortably thick. Damiano was leaving. Again. And he clearly had no intention of giving him any promises. Again.

"It is," he said tersely, unable to meet his eyes.

"It looks like yours," Damiano said in a strange voice.

Jordan nodded, looking at his own ring. "They're from the same batch, so they're similar in design. Our family company specializes in mini gadgets, and this one is basically a very sophisticated GPS tracker."

He felt rather than saw Damiano tense up. "A tracker?"

"Yeah," Jordan said. "Look, I know what you're thinking, but it's not—it's not that I want to track you and control you—it's..."

His throat constricted. "I hate not knowing where you are," he admitted, without looking at Damiano. "I hate the anxiety when you don't call for days, hate wondering if something happened to you. It's not like anyone would tell me if something did happen. I'm no one to you. So I thought—I thought I could give you one of these. It's really useful—we might have been found sooner if we had one of these rings on us when we were kidnapped."

Silence fell.

"How many people have access to the tracker?"

"Only me," Jordan said. "I removed it from the family's file system." He shrugged, putting his hands into his pockets. "I'm a programmer. It was five minutes' work—"

"Jordan"

Jordan's stomach clenched. He looked up.

Damiano was frowning deeply at the ring in his hands before looking back at Jordan. "This would be a huge security risk," he said. "I can't accept it. Lorenzo would have my head."

Right.

Of course. Of course Damiano wouldn't accept his gift. He didn't know what he had been thinking… Damiano wasn't the type of man to allow anyone to track his whereabouts; he was too paranoid for that. Of course he wouldn't consent to it.

"Never mind," Jordan said, taking the ring and turning away.

A hand grabbed his arm and turned him around. "It's stupid to feel upset," Damiano said in a clipped voice. "You know me. I can't accept such a security risk."

"I'm not upset," Jordan lied with a crooked smile. "It's fine."

Damiano glared, his expression tight. "You're lying. I know you."

Yes. He knew him. That was the problem. Damiano might lack empathy when it came to other people, but he never lacked it when it came to him. They both were so attuned to each other that anything other than honesty was pointless.

"Maybe I am upset," Jordan admitted with a humorless smile. "A little bit. But yeah, I knew the chances of you accepting this gift were slim at best. It's—it's okay. Go. I'll get over it."

Damiano's jaw worked.

Seconds dragged as Jordan looked at Damiano's coat and Damiano looked at him.

"Fine," Damiano ground out. "Give me the ring. I'll wear the damn thing if it makes you stop looking like this."

Jordan blinked, his mouth falling open. "Really?"

"Yes."

Beaming at him, Jordan retrieved the ring from its box, took Damiano's left hand and pushed the ring on his ring finger.

His mouth dry, he admired it for a moment. The platinum ring was thick and masculine, but fairly simple and unobtrusive, with simple geometric engravings that matched the ones on Jordan's own ring. It looked better on Damiano's darker finger than it did on Jordan's pale one.

"Thanks," Jordan murmured, pressing his matching ring against Damiano's. "I won't tell anyone your whereabouts, I swear."

"That isn't what I'm worried about," Damiano said.

When Jordan glanced up at him, he found Damiano staring at their fingers with an odd expression.

God, he was so heart-stoppingly handsome.

Jordan couldn't get enough of looking at him, at his dark hair covered in snowflakes, his perfectly sculpted eyebrows, penetrating eyes, and firm, sensual lips. His broad shoulders were practically begging to be touched, to be hugged.

Damiano lifted his gaze from their hands and met his eyes. Then, he yanked him close and kissed him hard, his hands cradling Jordan's face in a firm, possessive grip, his mouth hot and perfect, a stark contrast to the cold snowflakes falling on his face.

By the time Damiano released him, Jordan couldn't tell left from right, the world a distant blur, Damiano's face the only thing in focus.

They gazed at each other in silence, both of them panting.

*Don't go*, Jordan wanted to say.

*Come back to me*, he wanted to say.

*I love you*, he wanted to say.

He said nothing, the words getting stuck somewhere in his throat, like a painful lump.

His eyes wide, he could only watch as Damiano turned around and walked away.

Three bodyguards appeared out of nowhere, following Damiano to the waiting car.

They got in. Damiano paused for a moment, with his back to Jordan, before getting in the car too.

The car took off.

And Jordan was alone, again.

# Chapter 26

Jordan got drunk once he got home. He wasn't proud of it, but there was an awful sinking feeling in his stomach that wouldn't go away. He wasn't even sure why he felt so upset and heartbroken. It was fucking stupid. It wasn't as though Damiano had ever promised him something. In fact, he had told him several times that he wasn't capable of committing to anyone, that it was a weakness he would never allow himself. Jordan had known that.

It didn't hurt any less.

"Merry Christmas to me," he said with a laugh, taking another swig from his bottle of vodka. And then another, and another, and another.

He didn't sleep. Or maybe he did. He wasn't sure. The sky was light already, so it was probably morning.

There was music coming from somewhere. Wait. Was it his ringtone? Where was his phone?

The world was shaking funnily as Jordan looked for it. Miraculously, his phone was still ringing by the time he found it. It must have been someone very patient. Or maybe it was some stubborn, inconsiderate asshole who didn't care that people might be busy or asleep.

It was the latter, Jordan realized as he squinted at the Caller ID. Raffaele Ferrara.

"What do you want?" he snapped. Slurred. Whatever.

There was a pause. "Are you drunk?" his boss said.

"Maybe," Jordan said, falling back onto the couch. His arms didn't support his weight for some reason. "What is it to you?"

"Wow, he really is drunk," another voice said, sounding stunned. It was Nate. They must have had him on speaker.

Fuck that. He didn't care. Fuck them, and fuck their nauseatingly happy life. They were the reason he was getting drunk on Christmas all alone, like the worst sort of loser. If it weren't for Raffaele and Nate, he would have never met Damiano. He would have gone on with his life, having no idea that he even existed.

The thought only made him feel worse.

Fuck, he hated this.

Ferrara cleared his throat. "I see it's not a good time. We won't take your time—I was just wondering if you saw Damiano. He turned up at our house for Christmas and then disappeared without a word for days. I'm worried he's up to something."

Up to something.

How dare he. Instead of being worried for his stepbrother, Ferrara was worried that he was *up to something*.

Jordan curled a hand into a fist. "Fuck you," he ground out, suddenly fed up. His chest hurt. His throat hurt. His vision was blurry. "This is all your fault. It's your fault that—that he's the way he is. If—if you and your gang of privileged little boys treated him normally, if you were his friend—he wouldn't have—he wouldn't have turned out the way he is. Lonely. Unloved. Unable to trust. Unable to accept love."

There was dead silence on the line.

Jordan's lips twisted. It seemed even the great and terrible Raffaele Ferrara could be rendered speechless. Jordan was probably going to regret saying all of that tomorrow—he *was* drunk—but he didn't care. He wasn't scared of his boss. Even if Ferrara fired him, with his resume, he could easily find another job. In fact...

"I quit," Jordan said with relish, and hung up.

All the fight left him as he let his phone fall, hot tears falling down his cheeks.

Fuck, he was such a mess.

He was a mess without him.

He didn't want to ever be without him.

*Then what are you doing, getting drunk on Christmas, instead of getting the man?*

Jordan sat up, blinking blearily.

That was... a very reasonable question, actually. Why was he waiting for *Damiano* to come back? Why? Jordan could go after what he wanted, too. Especially since he wasn't the emotionally stunted one between the two of them. Damiano was... he wasn't built like that. He wasn't built to believe that he could be happy, that he could love and be loved back. Damiano would not be able to say the words easily. He might not be able to say them *ever*.

If Jordan kept waiting for Damiano to profess his undying love for him, he might have to endure decades of this uncertainty, with Damiano appearing and disappearing from his life, looking at Jordan longingly but never staying, until they both were old and gray.

Fuck that.

Words didn't matter.

Actions spoke louder than any words. And fuck, Damiano's actions spoke better than any *I love yous*. He'd let Jordan put a *ring* on him, for fuck's sake.

A ring that could track Damiano's whereabouts anywhere in the world. There was no bigger sign of trust Damiano could have possibly given him, considering how paranoid he normally was.

Damiano loved him. He had to believe that.

The only thing that stood between them and what they both wanted was themselves.

***

Jordan drank a lot of water, took a hot shower, freshened his breath, shaved, combed his hair, dressed up—put himself in order.

He was half-afraid his resolve would falter once he sobered up, but it didn't happen. He was sure. He was sure it was the right thing to do. He'd never been more sure in his life.

Damiano's GPS tracker showed that he was already in Italy, somewhere in Sicily, so Jordan booked the next available flight—which was an overnight flight that evening—and made himself busy.

He took a cab to work and left his letter of resignation. He was a little relieved that it was the holidays and there was no one at the office: he knew he still wasn't entirely sober and probably looked it.

After that, Jordan forced himself to call Ferrara. He really didn't want to do it, but it was the smart thing to do, professionally. He wasn't exactly giving Ferrara two weeks' notice, after all.

"Look, I'm sorry," he said once the man picked up. "I was out of line."

Ferrara sighed. "No," he said. His voice sounded clipped but not insincere.

"You weren't wrong. I am sorry—for all of it. I know I was part of the problem."

"You were," Jordan said, without venom this time. He still felt fiercely protective of Damiano and angry on his behalf, but he also knew Ferrara wasn't really a malicious sort of asshole—just a regular one, who hadn't meant for it to turn out this way.

"Are you really quitting?" Ferrara said after a pause.

"Yes. I know it's sudden and I have to give you two weeks to find a replacement, but…"

"It's fine," Ferrara said, just as Jordan knew he would.

He smiled to himself. Compared to dealing with Damiano, Ferrara was so easy to read and manipulate. "Thanks. I'm leaving for Italy, so if you or my replacement have any work-related questions, you can call me."

"Are you sure?" Ferrara said.

Jordan knew he wasn't asking about whether he was sure that they could call him if they had questions.

"I am," he said.

"That life isn't easy," Ferrara said. "I left it behind for a reason. Did you really think it through?"

Jordan licked his lips and thought about it. During their captivity, Damiano had told him a little about why his stepbrother had left Italy, about the toxic atmosphere in the Ferrara household caused by Raffaele's drunkard mother and cheating father on top of the usual stress that came from being the heir to the family business.

"You were running from something," Jordan said quietly. "I'm running toward something. That's the difference. I can put up with a lot for him." *I can't bear a life without him in it.*

Ferrara was silent for a while before chuckling. "Tell Damiano I expect a small island with a thank you note from him as my Christmas gift."

Jordan rolled his eyes. "You're such an asshole. You had nothing to do with this."

"I'm the one who introduced you."

"You have a strange definition for 'introduced,'" Jordan said with a snort, but he found himself smiling. He did like his boss—when he wasn't being an asshole to Damiano. "I have to go. Tell Nate I said hi."

"Hi yourself," Nate said.

Apparently he had been on speaker all along. Again.

"Hi," Jordan said with a laugh and hung up.

His smile slipped as he put his phone into his pocket.

For all his resolve, he was far from certain about how Damiano would react when he turned up in Italy without warning.

He might be royally pissed off.

Or worse—he might be unhappy.

# Chapter 27

By the time Jordan arrived at the house Damiano was supposed to be in, it was late morning. He didn't feel hungover anymore, but he was tired and cranky after the overnight transatlantic flight and then the flight from Rome to Sicily. Thankfully, the cool December air made him feel a lot better. It was nowhere near as cold as it had been in Boston, but the air was refreshingly cool and the view was amazing. It was such a beautiful place, the gentle sea breeze adding a touch of salt to the vibrant air.

Jordan breathed deeply, looking up at the big white house on the hill, before walking to the gate, his suitcase's wheels very loud on the ancient cobblestones.

He could see the security guards watching him carefully as he approached, but thankfully, they didn't shoot on sight, which he had been half-afraid of.

One of the guards stepped forward, a hand on his holster, and said something in Italian. Was his tone menacing?

Jordan cleared his throat. "Hello. I'd like to talk to Lorenzo if he's here."

The man frowned but pulled out his phone. He said something into it—Jordan really needed to learn Italian one of these days—and then told Jordan in heavily accented English, "Wait here."

So he waited.

After what seemed like forever, Lorenzo walked out of the gate. His stoic face changed when he saw Jordan, though Jordan didn't know him well enough to judge if it was a bad change or a good change.

"Hey," Jordan said, feeling awkward as he suddenly remembered that the last time he saw Lorenzo the guy had bought ointment for his sore ass. Talk about awkward.

"Hello," Lorenzo said, his brows drawing close. There was some wariness in his body language, as if Jordan was the dangerous one with the gun between the two of them. Lorenzo glanced at Jordan's suitcase. "What are you doing here?"

"I want to see him. Tell them I can be trusted to go inside."

Lorenzo gave him a flat look.

"Can you be trusted?"

Jordan had always gotten the feeling that Lorenzo didn't exactly approve of Damiano's relationship with him, and this confirmed it.

"I can be," Jordan said, looking him in the eyes. "We're on the same side here. You don't need to protect him from me."

Lorenzo studied him for a long moment, his gaze unreadable. "You could have called him and told him you were here."

"I want to surprise him," Jordan said.

It was only part of the truth. He was half-afraid that Damiano would be angry and turn him away, not wanting to be associated with him so openly. The dirty little secrets weren't supposed to walk up to his home in the middle of the day, after all.

Lorenzo's face was still like stone.

"Please," Jordan said. It didn't come easily to him. It wasn't a word he used often.

Thankfully, it seemed to work—Lorenzo's face softened a little. "Let's go," he said curtly and said something to the guards in Italian.

Jordan hurried after him, taking in his surroundings. This villa was majestic, but at the same time it looked more comfy and intimate than the one in Tivoli. There was a certain quality to it that stole Jordan's breath away. It was peaceful here. Beautiful but wild and lonely. The gardens here weren't groomed to perfection.

"It's his home, isn't it?" Jordan said, looking at the still pond.

"It's his main place of residence, yes," Lorenzo said. "He doesn't entertain guests and family here. How long are you staying for?"

Jordan's stomach clenched. "I don't know yet," he said. "Why are you asking?"

"I need to know how long he'll be distracted from work," Lorenzo said, scoffing.

"Are you saying I'm bad for him?"

Lorenzo shrugged.

"Not sure yet." His lips thinned. "I hope you know what you're doing. If you decide to stick around, there will be no going back. He's not the sort of man to ever allow that."

Jordan licked his dry lips and laughed a little. "You won't scare me away. I know him."

His face grim, Lorenzo shook his head. "He's a different man when he's with you—a better man. You've never seen him at his worst and nastiest. People fear him for a reason. He cares for you more than he's ever cared for anyone. It scares me."

A shiver ran up Jordan's spine. Maybe Lorenzo's words should have scared him. But they didn't. It felt good to have another person, someone who knew Damiano well, confirm that he cared a lot for Jordan, no matter how twisted and intense that devotion was. It didn't scare Jordan; it exhilarated him. Sometimes he was afraid that his feelings were one-sided, that Damiano couldn't possibly need him as badly as Jordan needed him. So Lorenzo's words only reassured him, no matter how messed up it might be.

"You have nothing to be scared of," Jordan said. "I have no intention of ever leaving him."

Lorenzo shook his head, his expression pinched. "You haven't seen the ugly side of him. You might walk out. Or someone might kill you. Or kidnap you. Or rape you. Or—"

"Wow, thanks," Jordan said with a laugh. "That's the sort of pep talk I needed—not. Relax, buddy."

Lorenzo heaved a sigh, running a hand through his hair. "I just worry."

"I worry for him, too," Jordan said, more softly. It was good to talk to someone who genuinely cared about Damiano too. No matter what Damiano might think, Lorenzo clearly was loyal to him. "I have no delusions. I know what he's capable of. I know he's not a good man. I know he's capable of killing in cold blood. Maybe it should scare me, but it doesn't. I feel safe—the safest—with him."

Lorenzo eyed him for a moment before nodding. For the first time ever, Jordan could see something like approval in his gaze.

"He's in his office," Lorenzo said, gesturing toward the door ahead.

Swallowing, Jordan headed toward it.

He stopped in front of it, trying to quash his doubt and uncertainty.

Then he pushed the door open.

***

Damiano didn't lift his eyes from his computer when he heard the door open. It was probably Lorenzo, back to nag him into eating. He didn't feel like eating.

He glanced down at the thick ring on his finger and his stomach clenched.

He'd had the ring for almost two days, but it was still extremely distracting, its heavy weight like a brand. Every time he looked at it, his chest filled with a sensation not unlike drowning but much more pleasant. Jordan had given it to him. Jordan was wearing a matching one. The thought was like a snake, coiling around all his thoughts, poisoning them with overwhelming possessiveness. For the first time, Damiano understood the appeal of wedding rings.

"Hey."

Damiano went rigid, his eyes snapping upward. For a moment, he thought he had lost his mind and started hallucinating. Because there was Jordan leaning against the door.

Jordan smiled crookedly. "Why are you looking at me like I'm a ghost?"

He really was here. In his home.

"What are you doing here?" Damiano heard himself say.

Jordan pushed away from the door and walked to Damiano.

"Hi there," he said, placing his hand on the back of Damiano's chair and leaning down. His blue eyes looked hesitant. "You look like you're unhappy to see me."

Damiano inhaled deeply, taking a lungful of his familiar scent.

Unhappy? It wasn't the emotion he was feeling.

"What are you doing here?" he repeated, his hands settling on Jordan's waist. To steady him. Not because he needed to touch him. It had been just two days, for fuck's sake. He wasn't that pathetic.

Jordan's dark gold brows furrowed, something uncertain about his expression as his gaze roamed over Damiano's.

Christ, he wanted to devour him, bite his pink, beautiful lips, crawl under his skin and eat him from the inside, find out what he tasted like, what his warmth tasted like. Damiano could almost taste it on the back of his tongue, and he nearly choked on the saliva pooling in his mouth.

His hands tugged Jordan into his lap, of their own volition. Jordan allowed him, straddling his thighs. Their chests brushed together. Damiano wondered if Jordan could feel how hard his heart was pounding.

"I'm here because..." Jordan locked his eyes with his. "I'm here because I can't do this anymore, Damiano."

Something lodged into his throat. "And you came all the way to Italy to tell me that?"

Jordan sighed and threaded his fingers through Damiano's hair, the touch unbearably gentle. It sent a shudder through him. He wanted more, but he forced himself not to lean into the touch.

He glowered at Jordan.

What was he playing at?

"Why do you always assume the worst?" Jordan said, brushing his fingertips against Damiano's eyebrows. "Stop frowning so much. Though I guess your stupidly handsome face would benefit from a few wrinkles. I'm looking forward to them."

"I—I do not understand." At times like this, he thought his grasp of English wasn't sufficient.

Jordan smiled at him, his blue eyes so very soft and pretty. "How can such an intelligent man be so dumb when it comes to feelings? I can't live without you, you dummy. And I'm done with your hot-and-cold act. You don't get to treat me like that, coming and going out of my life as you please. Fuck that. You're stuck with me from now on."

There was a strange feeling in his chest, unbearable in its intensity. He was possibly suffocating—his throat felt too tight, as well. Perhaps he had been poisoned. It wouldn't be the first time.

"You can't," he managed. "It's dangerous, with who I am. You might die."

Jordan shrugged. "That's true. But I might die in Boston too. I might get hit by a bus and die tomorrow. Life is a risk. And it's one worth taking. I'd rather die happy with the man I love than miserable and alone."

*With the man I love.*

*With the man I love.*

*With the man I love.*

Jordan cradled his face with his hands and smiled. "You look like you've been hit by a truck. Surely you had an inkling about my feelings for you? I wasn't exactly subtle. But I get it—it's different to hear the words, isn't it?" He stroked Damiano's cheekbones with his thumbs. "God, I love you so much. I didn't know it was possible to love someone so much."

He smiled crookedly. "You'd better feel the same way or I don't know what I'd do. I might cry. I'm such a mess without you, it's embarrassing."

Damiano tried to swallow around the thickness in his throat. When it didn't work, he had to clear it a few times. He wanted to ask if Jordan was sure. He wanted to *make* him say it again. He wanted to tell Jordan that he wasn't allowed to ever change his mind. But what left his mouth was, "Ten bodyguards."

"Huh?"

"You will have at least ten bodyguards with you all the time."

Jordan stared at him. And then he laughed. "You can just say it, you know. Say that you love me. Surely you aren't scared of a word?"

Damiano had to clear his throat again. "I don't—I don't know if what I feel for you is love."

"Oh." The light in Jordan's eyes dimmed, and Damiano *hated* it. He wanted those blue eyes to be alight with affection, always. He was addicted to the way Jordan looked at him—as if he were worth loving. As if he were a better man than he was. He wasn't. Frankly, people weren't wrong when they called him unfeeling, selfish, and heartless. He didn't care about people. Most people were just tools for him. He felt no remorse about hurting people. Except this one. This one was precious. This one was his. This one made him feel.

"I don't know how 'love' is supposed to feel," Damiano said, struggling to hold Jordan's gaze. He'd never felt more off-balance in his life—he'd never been good at admitting being bad at anything. "I know that I—that I care for you."

*Care* seemed such a weak, inadequate word.

English had never seemed more difficult for him. Or maybe the language barrier wasn't to blame. There weren't adequate words to convey what he was feeling even in Italian. "I feel…"

Jordan made an encouraging noise, looking at him earnestly.

Damiano felt his ears turn hot. "Love is always depicted as a nice, sweet feeling in the movies. What I feel for you isn't sweet. It isn't nice. Sometimes I almost hate you for turning me into this. For making me—for making me need another person. For wanting to be a better person than I am. I don't like it—the way you make me feel."

"What way?" Jordan said, his gaze very soft.

"Unbalanced and distracted—when you aren't around. Obsessive, possessive, and out of control when you are. If this is love, it fucking sucks."

Jordan smiled.

"Love doesn't have to be like in the movies," he murmured, stroking Damiano's cheek with his thumb. "Everyone loves differently. I think you're doing pretty great for an emotionally stunted asshole."

Damiano wrapped his arms around him. "But is it enough for you?" The words were hard to say. His throat felt like sandpaper.

*Am I enough?*

Jordan looked at him seriously.

"It is," he said, his voice soft. "I'd prefer your fucked-up version of love to the sweetest, most conventional love lavished on me by another person. Because it's you. And you're more than enough. You're what I need to feel enough."

Damiano tightened his arms.

"I'll do better," he said roughly. "I'll try for you."

Jordan grinned. "And you say your feelings aren't sweet. I think they're plenty sweet. I turned you into a cuddler. I can turn you into a certified sap in… let's say a year."

A year.

It was hard to believe that he—they—were talking talking about the future. Their future.

"You're staying here, right?" Damiano said, clearing his throat. "Indefinitely." Forever. Jordan would be his forever.

Jordan shrugged, looking at him curiously. "That was the plan, yeah. I even quit my job."

Damiano just nodded, trying not to show how pleased he felt. A better man would probably object to Jordan leaving his old life for him. He wasn't a better man.

"Your family will need bodyguards too," Damiano said.

"Why?" Jordan said, blinking. "You don't care for them."

"But you do."

Jordan stared at him.

"You *are* sweet," he said, his voice a little choked up.

Before Damiano could say that his decision to give Jordan's family bodyguards had nothing to with him being "sweet" and everything to do with his unwillingness to be blackmailed, Jordan cradled his face. "God, I love you," he said, and kissed him.

Damiano kissed back, his mind clouding with want and his heart lurching at those words. *I love you*, he tried them in his mind. They didn't feel wrong. *Ti amo*. They didn't feel wrong, either. In fact, he almost wanted to say them. But he didn't want to say them before he was sure. Jordan deserved better.

But that didn't mean he couldn't hear the words. "Say it again," he ordered against Jordan's lips.

Jordan grinned. "I love you," he said between kisses. "I love you, I love you, I love you."

Every word filled the deep, hungry pit in his chest that Damiano hadn't even known existed.

Feeling almost intoxicated, Damiano put Jordan on his desk and pushed him under him.

Where he belonged.

*I love you.*

He might not have been able to say the words, but he could show it.

He would very much enjoy showing it.

# Epilogue

*One year later*

Jordan hugged his sister tightly.

"Let me look at you!" Eloise said, pulling back and grinning. "You look so tan!"

"Living in Sicily would do it," Jordan said dryly.

"Where's your worse half?" Eloise said, craning her neck, as if she expected Damiano to be hiding behind him.

"He'll be here soon." Jordan rolled his eyes. "He's getting wine for Dad. The wine we brought with us got broken in transit."

"Ouch," Eloise said, taking his arm, and walking toward the house. "The kids will be so happy to see you. They missed you. We all did."

"I missed you guys too," Jordan said softly, looking at his parents' house festively decorated for Christmas. "I'm sorry we missed Christmas dinner, but Damiano has a big family and we had to spend Christmas with them."

Strictly speaking, they didn't *have* to spend Christmas with Damiano's family, but Jordan had insisted. He'd been gradually convincing Damiano to act friendlier with the clan instead of ruling them with fear. It was slow going, but Jordan was satisfied with the progress so far.

There were already a few relatives he could legitimately call friends and who didn't piss themselves every time Damiano frowned.

"I get it," his sister said. "How is business?"

"Good," Jordan said. The game development studio that he'd founded in Italy had been doing a little too well, in fact. So well that Jordan had a sneaking suspicion Damiano was helping it take off, even though he'd denied it.

"What about your personal life?" Eloise said.

Jordan found himself smiling. "Great. We're great."

They *were* great. More than great. It wasn't that he and Damiano didn't have disagreements or fights; they did. They both were stubborn and too set in their own ways to not butt heads from time to time, especially when it came to Damiano's overprotectiveness. But the good far outweighed the bad, and Damiano was very sweet and considerate after their fights. Not to mention that the makeup sex was amazing. To be fair, all sex with Damiano was amazing.

"Is Mom going to be okay with Damiano?" Jordan said, changing the subject before his body could react to those thoughts.

Eloise squeezed his arm. "It's going to be fine, don't worry about it. Any doubts she had about your Italian mafioso are nothing compared to the fact that he got Aiden back. Right now Damiano is probably her favorite person in the world."

Jordan smiled. "I know. I still can't believe Damiano found him."

It had been as much of a surprise to him as it had been for their parents. Damiano had kept quiet about his search for Jordan's missing brother until after he found him in Dubai. Jordan had been so happy, of course—until he found out about Aiden's fate: he'd been living in some rich sheikh's household. Jordan had *known* that sex trafficking could be the reason for his brother's disappearance: Aiden's exquisite looks might have attracted the wrong sort of attention. But suspecting something and knowing were two different things.

"How is he?" Jordan said.

Eloise shrugged, her expression turning grimmer. "Putting on a happy face, but I can sense that something is off. I don't think he's as happy to be saved as he pretends to be."

Jordan frowned. "He probably just needs time."

"I don't know," his sister said. "It's been months already. He isn't getting better and he still refuses to talk or file charges against the sheikh. He claims that nothing happened, but I find it hard to believe. Maybe it's some fucked-up Stockholm Syndrome."

"Yeah," Jordan said, but his attention was already drifting away as Damiano's car rolled to a stop in the driveway.

"Your man certainly travels in style," Eloise said, whistling. "Sweet ride. Though I could have done without dozens of bodyguards on the front lawn. They ruin the view."

Jordan chuckled distractedly, watching Damiano emerge out of the car.

"One might think you haven't seen him in days instead of half an hour," his sister said, laughing. "Jesus, your heart-eyes are embarrassing for a grown man."

"You're just jealous," Jordan said.

"I am," she admitted with a grin. "Wish Paul made me look at him like this."

Jordan felt his face become warm. He hated being this obvious, but he could never control his expressions when it came to Damiano. And truth be told, he didn't try very hard. He knew Damiano loved the affection and the adoration—he greedily soaked it up, no matter what he might claim otherwise. So Jordan didn't restrain himself. Damiano deserved all the love in the world.

"Eloise," Damiano said, pecking her on the cheek.

Jordan beamed at him proudly. A year ago, Damiano would have never done such a thing.

He grabbed Damiano's hand as soon as his sister let go of him and entwined their fingers together. "Well done," he whispered, kissing him on the stubbled cheek and inhaling his masculine scent.

Damiano quirked a dark eyebrow. "I can pretend to be normal, you know."

Jordan glared at him, gently stroking his coat lapel. "*You're* normal," he said, darting forward to steal a kiss. "Just the way you are. Pretending to be polite doesn't make you normal—it just makes you seem less aloof, which is our aim."

"Aye-aye, sir," Damiano said with a wry, heart-stopping smile, and Jordan just had to steal another kiss. And then another. *Mmm.*

"I love you," Jordan murmured against his lips.

Damiano pulled him closer and whispered, "I love you, too." There was still a certain hesitance in his voice when he said it, as if he was getting away with something every time he said those words, as if he couldn't possibly deserve to love and to be loved, and Jordan hugged him tightly and kissed him deeper, his heart so full with adoration and love that he was almost choking on it.

"Jesus, Jord, get a room!"

Grinning sheepishly, Jordan pulled back and looked at Damiano, who didn't even glance at Eloise, his eyes only on Jordan, soft and glassy with want.

God, he loved him.

Cradling his stubbled cheek, Jordan stole another quick kiss, before heading toward his parents' house, hand in hand with the man he loved.

*The End*

# About the Author

Alessandra Hazard is the author of the bestselling MM romance series *Straight Guys*, *The Wrong Alpha*, *Calluvia's Royalty*.

Visit Alessandra's website to learn more about her books: http://www.alessandrahazard.com/books/

To be notified when Alessandra's new books become available, you can subscribe to her mailing list: http://www.alessandrahazard.com/subscribe/

You can contact the author at her website or email her at author@alessandrahazard.com.